Shaun Meeks is the author of the Dillon the Monster Dick series (*The Gate at Lake Drive, Earthbound and Down,* and *Altered Gates*), as well as *Shutdown, Down on the Farm,* and upcoming release, Maymon. He has published over 50 short stories, the most recent appearing in *Midian Unmade, Zippered Flesh 3, The Best of the Horror Zine, Dark Moon Digest, Rogue Nation,* and *Fresh Fear*. His short stories have been collected in *From Nightmares, Dreams, Dark Reaches, Brother's Ilk (with James Meeks), At the Gates of Madness,* and the upcoming *Blood on the Ground: Six Shots of Southern Discomfort*. This year Shaun is working on the fifth novel in the Dillon series, two standalone novels (*The Place Where the Shadows Live,* and *The Desolate*) Shaun currently lives in Toronto, Ontario with his partner, and their micro-yeti, Lily, where they are always planning the next adventure. To find out more or to contact Shaun, please visit www.shaunmeeks.com, www.facebook.com/shaunmeeks, or www.twitter.com/ShaunMeeks

Shaun Meeks' Dillon the Monster Dick series published by IFWG Publishing International

The Gate at Lake Drive (Book 1, 2015)
Earthbound and Down (Book 2, 2017)
Altered Gate (Book 3, 2019)
Heads, You Lose (Book 4, 2022)

Book 4:
Dillon the Monster Dick series

Heads, You Lose

by
Shaun Meeks

Heads, You Lose

ISBN-13: 978-1-922556-72-1

V1.0

Printed in Palatino Linotype and Arno Pro.

IFWG Publishing International
Gold Coast

www.ifwgpublishing.com

Acknowledgements

As always, there are so many people to thank when putting out a book. First, I want to thank Gerry Huntman and everyone at IFWG Publishing who work so hard and allow me to write these books the way they are, allowing my voice to stay as it is, even when some might think the ideas are too strange. I also want to give a huge thanks to Steve Santiago, whose cover art has lifted these books up and who manages to always come up with exactly what I envisage.

There are also the police officers in Toronto who I've worked closely with over the last twenty years. So many of them have helped with the technical aspects and showing me so much of what really goes on in law enforcement. I won't say their names, but they know who they are, especially all the ones in 51 Division.

Not only did the police help me with this stuff, but so many people I worked with over the years. I've been at my job for nearly twenty years now, working in some of the roughest areas of the city, and I've been lucky enough to have some great partners who helped inspire many of the characters in here. Whether it's just their name, or little things that make up their character, I've had such a blast with so many of them that I felt they needed to be in this series, one way or another. Thank you all for being my backup, and a source of inspiration.

Over the years I've worked with so many helpful and amazing editors who not only polished my writing, but gave me so much advice to make me become a better writer. A huge thanks to Jeani Rector, Weldon Burge, Lori Michelle, Stephen McCracken, Sophie Yorkston, and Noel Osualdini, just to name a few.

And of course, a huge thanks to my love and my partner, Gillian. You listen so well to my madness, let me bounce ideas and plot lines off of you, and never let me get away with anything that might just be skating by. You always help me to be a better writer and person.

This book is dedicated to Brenda Ansara (aka Mrs A). You were the first person who really believed in my writing, encouraged me to pursue this crazy life. I can't thank you enough.

Friday

The puppy was stealing some of the fallen pizza as I stood over Don Parks and watched the pool of blood under him grow larger. There was a part of me that was sure he was going to get up any minute, jump up and charge at me, even though when I saw Rouge pull the knife from him, I knew he was dead. It was an irrational thought, but there it was. I guess I've watched too many horror movies over the years. How many times had I seen Freddy, Jason, and Chucky do it? How many times had I seen them killed, sometimes brutally, only to rise up as determined as ever to continue the carnage? More times than I can remember. It was a trope I hated, but standing over the dead man, I couldn't help but expect it to happen in that moment.

"Hey, Dillon," Rouge said, pulling me from my thoughts with a jolt.

"What?" I asked, keeping my eyes on the Don's body.

"Can I keep the knife?"

I turned to her, reluctant to take my eyes off the hunter in case he somehow managed to survive, but I needed to see if Rouge was serious. I couldn't believe she was taking it all in stride, and possibly cracking jokes. I was still full of adrenaline from the short fight, could still feel the weight of Don Parks on me, and here she was asking to keep the knife.

"Why do you want it?" I finally asked, seeing that she wasn't joking.

"Well, if I'm going to join you and be a hunter too, I think I'm going to need a knife like yours. I assume this one has all the same bells and whistles yours does."

"Let me see it," I said, and held out my hand, trying not to notice how it was shaking. Reluctantly, Rouge passed me the knife, the same one the dead hunter had been about to plunge into me. The hilt was warm, and I could instantly see there were thin, intricately carved symbols and words of alien origin etched into it and the blade. It was very much like the Tincher I carried. I nodded and handed it back to her. "It seems to. Are you sure you want it?"

"Well, I think if I'm going to do what you do; I'm going to need to have something like this, don't you?"

I nodded, but I still wasn't sure. Rouge seemed very insistent about being by my side in the work I did, and she'd more than proved herself by killing Don Parks. Not to mention what she did in Niagara Falls, but I was still worried. My concern wasn't just for her safety, but for the ramifications that might come from breaking more rules than ever before. I didn't feel as though I needed to be there to protect her from anything, but I didn't want to be the one to help her step off the cliff either. I had no idea how the Collective would react to her hunting at my side. There was a good chance it would be the straw that broke the camel's back. One thing I was pretty sure about was there'd be some sort of fallout over her killing a hunter.

Only time would tell.

"I guess you're right," I agreed, handed her the blade, and looked at her as she admired it in the low light.

"So what do we do about him?" she asked, pointing at the bloody mess as the puppy walked over and sniffed at the spreading red puddle. "Oh no, you silly thing. Get away from that. Someone that shitty, who knows how rotten that blood is." She scooped up the dog and asked me again what we should do about it.

"We need to take it to the bath tub," I told her. "You should put the dog in one of the rooms. I'm going to need your help."

She put the dog in her bedroom and shut the door. The little thing whined from inside as we hefted the body down the hall to the bathroom and put it in the tub. It was hard work, and we needed to take a few breaks, smearing blood on the hardwood floors as we went. It was a good thing Rouge's grandmother didn't have wall-to-wall carpets or the cleanup afterwards would have been a real horror.

When we finally got him in the bathroom, we lifted him into the tub, and I stripped the blood-soaked clothes off of the body. Once the hard work was done, I gave my hands a quick wash before going out to grab my bag. Rouge was standing outside of the bathroom, towel drying her own freshly washed hands when I got back, breathing heavily and looking a little green around the gills.

"Are you okay?" I asked and put a hand on her shoulder. She nodded, but she looked a little off. I'm sure a naked man dead in her tub wasn't anything she'd ever thought she'd see, and what I was going to do next wouldn't be any easier. I knew she wanted to be a part of what I did, but there was no point in throwing her right into the deep end before she even knew how to swim. "Why don't you go to the kitchen and clean up? I'll finish up in here."

"What are you going to do with…" she started, and then trailed off as her eyes went back to the bathroom's interior. I looked over and all you could see of Don was the top of his head, and his feet hanging out on either side of the tub.

"I have something that'll get rid of the body. It's not going to be a pretty sight, so maybe you go clean up the kitchen and hallway while I tend to this. If you don't mind, maybe you could put on the kettle, and we'll have some tea or coffee afterwards. Sound good?"

She nodded and left. I went into the bathroom with my bag and got to work. Even I wasn't looking forward to what came next, so I was glad she didn't need to be there for it. I know she's tough, but there are some things that aren't easy to get used to, and making Parks disappear was one of them.

I've watched movies where people have to dispose of bodies, and luckily my plan wasn't nearly as disgusting as any of that. There would be no sawing or cutting up his corpse; nothing as visceral as that. I didn't need a chainsaw or hacksaw for this job. Instead, I filled up the tub halfway with warm water, doing my best not to look down at Don Parks' body; especially his face. It's not the first dead body I've seen, obviously, but death is something I've never really gotten used to. I mean, does anyone of sound mind really enjoy the sight of a dead person in front of them? I hope not. Still, I had a job to do, and I could stomach it. Dispatching monsters is nothing compared to seeing a dead human—even if that human is just a host body for a hunter.

Once there was enough water, I shut the taps off, went into my bag, and pulled out a vial of cloudy, violet liquid. I've had it for a long time, since shortly after I arrived on Earth, but only used it one time previous. That time it wasn't to dispose of someone I–or anyone I was associated with–had killed. The only time previous was to dispose of a body I'd lost. Well, saying I lost it is an understatement. I'd gotten into a fight with a creature I'd been hunting for months. I lost round one by way of having my head torn off. Once I took a new body and recovered my equipment, I disposed of my old body the way I was about to dispose of Don Parks' corpse. That was something of a mind fuck. Seeing your own body and severed head, a face you've been looking at in the mirror for so many years, could easily shake someone who wasn't used to messed-up situations. Lucky for me, messed-up situations are sort of my specialty. Like that time, this would be fast, and smell like burnt hair and an open sewer, but at least there wouldn't be a body lying around I'd have to explain.

Four drops of the violet liquid were all it would take. The second the last drop hit, the water began to boil, and the body of the hunter who'd tried to kill me began to shrivel up, melting into a thick pool of purple and red. The smell was terrible, worse than I remembered it, and I turned on the bathroom exhaust and opened the window. It helped a little, but not enough, so I put a few drops of *Poo-Pourri* in the tub, figuring if it could cover up the aftermath of a four-bean chilli perhaps it would help with Don Parks soup, too. He had been a turd in a human body after all.

"I can smell that out here," Rouge called from the kitchen, and I apologized. I knew it wouldn't be much longer, and then we could air the place out properly.

I sat down on the closed toilet while waiting, feeling the last few days weighing down on me. My head gave the whispers of a headache from drugs I'd been given at the mental hospital, and the nasty curse which had been put on me by a demon attached to a small, wisp of a woman. I closed my eyes, memories of the disturbing things I'd seen recently swirling through the darkness of my mind. Melting faces, headless men, and the madness I felt lingered like the taste of bad meat, and the smell of Don Parks' melting flesh didn't help at all.

"Tea's ready," Rouge called out and I opened my eyes, half expecting to see the liquefied remains of the dead hunter rising from the slimy bath tub. It didn't happen. There was nothing left to come out. The body was gone. I put on a rubber glove and I unplugged the tub, sending his remains down into the sewer where it belonged. I gave the tub a good rinse, used bleach to make sure the last of the goop was gone. When I was satisfied, I tossed the glove into the trash. I went out to meet Rouge, have some tea, and try to add some normality to my life.

Saturday

I woke up the next day long after the sun had risen. I knew we still had things to do, mainly to get rid of Don Parks' car, which had to be somewhere close to the house. I'd found his keys in the pocket of his blood-soaked pants before we set them in the fireplace with the rest of his clothes to burn. I would've done it the night before, but after everything, I just didn't have the energy to do it.

After a quick breakfast, the two of us set out to dump his car. Rouge agreed to drive mine and I took his piece of crap. The idea was to take it down to one of the rougher areas of the city and leave it with the keys inside, knowing it would disappear easily. If this city is nothing else, it's predictable when it comes to crime. Leave something unattended for a second and someone else will come along to claim it as their own.

As we finished packing and went looking for Don's car, my phone rang. I didn't even check who it was, not wanting to deal with potential clients or the ongoing crank calls, which had been going on since the YouTube video went up. I had enough on my plate without adding to it. Yet when it rang a second, and then a third time, I pulled it out of my pocket to see who it was.

"Crank?" Rouge asked when she saw me look at the display.

"No. It's Garcia," I told her. I thought about hanging up, but seeing as he doesn't normally call me, I felt I needed to know what seemed so urgent. Especially since he had called back two more times.

"Hello?" I said as we walked along the street, on the lookout for our prize.

"You busy?"

"A bit, but I'm assuming this is urgent?"

"I'm just on scene at something a little, well, strange. I wanted to know if you could stop by so I could see what you think."

I let out a long sigh. I wanted to be able to help him. After everything he did to help me get out of the mental hospital, the least I could do was offer him something in return. He wasn't the type of person to call asking for this and that, so I figured if he said there was something strange going on, there really must be something bizarre afoot. Yet, I just had too much to do at the moment. I didn't want to leave Parks' car sitting around, raising questions, leading back to me or Rouge. It wasn't as though Don Parks was going to report it missing, or that someone he knew would file a missing person's report, but there was a chance a nosy neighbor might make a call to the police about the strange car that had been parked there for days. If the police showed up, who knew where that would lead them? The idea it could take them to Don Parks' apartment, and then the possibility it could turn a spotlight on me, well, I wasn't willing to let that happen.

"Is there any way this can wait a bit?" I asked. "I'm right in the middle of something."

There was a moment of silence, and then I could hear someone in the background calling out to Garcia. He'd clearly covered his phone as he spoke to whoever was close by, and I couldn't make out anything he was saying.

"Don't worry about it," he said, and I swear I could hear the disappointment in his voice. "I'm sure things will make sense once I put my head to it. If not, maybe I'll can call you later. Is that okay?"

"Of course, and sorry about this," I said, and almost went into the details, but I knew we didn't have time for that.

"No worries. My bad for assuming you weren't doing anything," he said and then hung up.

I put my phone in my pocket and Rouge asked what the call was about. I explained it and she nodded, asking if I was sure I shouldn't just go.

"We need to deal with this first. We can ditch the car around Moss Park or St. Jamestown, or somewhere else like that. Then I'll see what's got him so stressed that he took the time to call me. Is that his car?" I said, and pointed to a junker with a missing window; the same window Rouge had smashed out not all that long ago.

"It is."

"Finally," I said, and we walked over to move it, ready to be done with the whole thing. I jumped in the car and she took mine. We decided to take it to one of the *Green P* parking lots near Yonge and Bloor after we checked the internet and found numerous articles about how it was one of the worst garages for vehicle break-ins and thefts. I left the doors unlocked, even though the smashed window would have provided easy access. I then put the key on the seat, making it look as though someone absentminded might have just left it there, instead of it looking like a bait car the police had set up to catch criminals. When I left the garage, Rouge was parked on the street in my car, and we headed off to grab some well-deserved breakfast.

To avoid the crowds and people who might still recognize me from the video, we decided to go through a drive-thru. A *Tim Hortons* down near Cherry Street was the easiest one to get to. It is an industrial part of the city, not real full of people who comb the internet for anything other than adult websites. I figured we were safe.

And we were.

We ordered food, drove down to the lake, and ate. The day was nice. There was a cold breeze coming off the water, but the sun was bright and warm, so we unrolled our windows to let some fresh air in. It was one of the first quiet moments we'd had in so long, talking about just random boring things instead of monsters, demons, mental hospitals, or being a hunter. We just spoke about the puppy, new movies coming out, getting out of the city for a little vacation, and a pair of shoes Rouge really wanted to pick up soon. It would be so boring to everyone else, but in that moment, it was so relaxing and made me feel normal.

"Do you want to do something tonight?" she asked, and sipped at her tea. "I'm up for dinner out, or we can try the Swiss Chalet or pizza again; do a little Netflix and chill."

I was still chuckling at that when my phone rang. I'd already forgotten about Garcia.

I pulled it out, ready to answer, and felt my heart stutter a bit when it was not the detective's number on the screen, but Godfrey's. Normally I was the one calling him for things, unless there was a problem, or on the rare occasion where he had a client for me. Only the last time he had one of those, well, things didn't turn out in my favour. Still, I answered the call to see what it was, hoping for some good news.

"What's up, Godfrey?"

"Where are you, Dillon?"

I didn't answer. That didn't sound like the man who supplied me with weapons and tools. Godfrey had a very distinctive voice, one with a thick Jamaican accent, and this man using his phone sounded whiter than white bread. For the shortest of seconds I had no idea who it could be, but the mystery didn't last long. How could I have been so stupid?

"You thought you could just kill me and I'd go away? You should know better than that, Dillon."

"What do you want, Parks?" I all but growled into the phone.

"Parks?" Rouge whispered beside me, and I could see fear behind her eyes. Not sure why I didn't think he'd be back so easily or so soon. He was, after all, no different than I was: an alien borrowing human bodies. "How?"

I held up a hand to her and put my phone on speaker so she could hear the conversation.

"Well, let's start off with giving me back my knife. Once you do, I would really like to get back to where we were before your human whore snuck up behind me and killed that filthy body I was using. And, if you do that fast, I might let your friend here live. I may even leave him here untouched, though I can't say the same about that bitch you have. I've been thinking a lot about ways to make her pay for what she did to me. Such an inconvenience shouldn't go unpunished, but I might let her off with little more than a spanking."

"You're not going to touch her, and you're not going to do anything to Godfrey, either. You know the rules, and hurting either of them just to get me, well, I'm not sure the Collective would allow that. You'd be in more trouble than me. So maybe you just drop the idle threats. You like to play by the rules so much, I know you're not going to go do something that would make you no better than me."

Nothing from Parks, so I hoped I'd struck a nerve. He'd been sent here, according to him, because I'd violated the rules set out by the Collective. I was dating a human, killed an earthbound creature or two, and made a public spectacle out of myself. Those, in the eyes of the higher-ups, were big charges, even though I'd done far worse over the years and had never been punished for it. Yet, according to Parks, what I had done recently was bad enough for them to send another hunter to remove me from Earth. But there was no way they'd allow Parks to harm a human to get at me, or to even do anything to Godfrey. Even though Godfrey was a criminal, serving out a sentence on Earth to assist me and other hunters, there were still rules to follow; and one of those rules was that no hunter would harm or remove someone serving out a sentence here. Lucky for me, I guess.

"I'm sure the Collective would be fine with me bending a few rules here and there to get at you. Especially with how many they allowed you to get away with before they ever bothered to send anyone after you. Now, unless you want to listen to me take this criminal apart, piece by piece, you will tell me where you are so we can finish this. You're the only one who can save him, so tell me now, Dillon: Where are you?"

"No. I don't think I will tell you where I am, but I know where you are. See you soon, Parks."

I hung up and let out a long breath. I could feel tension in my shoulders, reaching into my head and pounding behind my eyes. There was panic there, not unlike what I felt when I was infected by a demon which had made me see Death. I steadied my breath as best I could, and tried to figure out what to do next. I knew he wasn't allowed to hurt Godfrey, but that didn't mean he wouldn't. Parks was nothing if not tenacious. He wouldn't stop until he did his job, or until I killed not just the human body he'd borrowed, but the very essence of what he truly was. I should have remembered that. We are both in the same boat, after all. Neither of us are from this world, just in borrowed bodies. Kill the one we're in, and we can move to another. How could I not have thought of that?

"You okay?" Rouge asked, and put her hand on my leg. I turned to her and gave a weak nod. She looked scared. I'm not sure I could blame her for that. The person she'd just killed the day before was already back and clearly looking to hurt or kill her.

"Everything will be fine," I said, though I wasn't convinced it would be. Parks had been bad enough to deal with before Rouge had saved my life and killed him. Death, even one as superficial as the kind he went through, has a way of changing a person. I know when I was killed and had to go to another body, I hunted down the creature which dispatched me, and made it pay. Slowly. I didn't doubt for a second that the ideas of revenge floating through Parks' head were the stuff of nightmares. So saying we'd be fine, it felt weak to me.

"What should we do now?" Rouge asked and I shrugged, not really knowing. I looked out the window, as though there was an answer out there, but all I saw was a place unknown to me. "Maybe we should run back to my place and get some things. He knows where I live, and if he's at Godfrey's, we're closer to my place than he is."

"You're right," I said and didn't waste any time. I quickly turned the car and drove out of the parking spot, heading back towards her house. "We can grab the pup, my bag, and anything else you need."

"What about your place?"

"I don't think there's any chance we can go there. I don't know if he'd go there or your place first, but I'm thinking mine as he's going to assume I have things I need there." It was the play *I* would make, after all. He might've already been at my place when he called me on Godfrey's phone, trying to make me panic and rush home; although, he could also be doing the same thing at Rouge's house. I knew we'd have to be careful no matter what.

"I have plenty of things in my bag though, enough to get us by and maybe kill Parks once and for all."

"You can actually kill him?"

"I think so. Hopefully I have something that will do the trick."

"How come what I did didn't kill him?"

"Blades like my Tincher and the dagger you have can wipe out certain beings, but not all. Clearly when you stabbed Parks, there wasn't a curse embedded in it that was able to do the job. I'm not surprised he wouldn't have a curse on his blade that could do much damage. But, we will find a way to end him before he can hurt you."

"Or Godfrey," Rouge said and I nodded, though I was worried for him already. Godfrey was a bastard who'd tricked me on more than one occasion, but a friend despite that, and I didn't want to see him hurt because of something I did.

We pulled up to her house, and rushed inside to get the things we needed. My bag was easy to find. It was still sitting on the kitchen table where I'd left it, and as Rouge went to get what she wanted, I rummaged through to see what was in there. I carry a lot of random items in that battered, leather bag, never knowing what I'll need at any given time. Some days it might be full of knives, coins from realms I'd never been to before, or vials of blood from demons I've personally killed. At other times there's little more in it than my gloves, Tincher, and snacks. Seeing how packed it was, I was glad it wasn't the latter, that it was still full from my trip to Niagara Falls. I just needed to try and remember what I could use to kill a Thrak, which was the species Don Parks was.

"You almost ready?" I called out, and zipped up my bag and went to the fridge to grab some food we could eat on the go.

"Almost," she called out to me from her room. "How many days do you think this will take?"

"Your guess is as good as mine. Try to keep it as light as you can. I don't want you to lose a lot of your stuff if we need to run and ditch bulky things."

"So, no rhinestone gowns, I'm guessing?" she called out, and

I could hear her chuckle. "Leggings and hoodies it is. I'll be a comfortable bad-ass."

"Can't wait to see that," I said, but then had to try not to think about it. This was business, not a time to have a little fantasy.

We were packed up and leaving within a few minutes. Rouge had a small rolling suitcase in one hand, and her little pup tucked in her other arm. I asked her if she was sure that would be enough clothes and she smiled wickedly at me.

"Not sure I need all that many with you around," she said with a wink and it was nice to have a little saucy moment when things seemed a bit stressful. "What about you? Aren't you going to need some clothes to change into?"

"Yeah, well, we can always buy some later. I have plenty of money at hand without needing to go back to my apartment for stuff."

"This is why you should just move in here, Dill. Then you wouldn't need to go to your apartment for anything."

"I know you're right. And we can talk about that when this is over too. We can figure that out once we get Parks out of our hair once and for all."

"Won't they just send someone else after you?"

I shrugged. I didn't want to think about that. It was bad enough thinking about Parks without considering it would never really end, that I would simply be on the run for the rest of my life. I had no idea how serious the Collective would take all this. Sure, they sent Parks after me, but I wasn't positive if he was just an over-achiever who was coming at me hard because that's who he was, or if they were done with me and all my rule-breaking.

What I had never considered, what came into my head at that moment, was the idea that Parks had nothing to do with the Collective at all. What if he was something else entirely? I'd been hearing so much lately about things being stirred up; a rebellion among realms, dimensions, and planets against the Collective. What if he was nothing more than another being coming after me the way the Hellion and the others had recently?

Then again, I could be just getting paranoid because of everything going on.

By the time we stepped back out and headed towards the car, the temperature had dropped and the sun was hiding behind some thick, grey clouds. I cautiously looked up and down the street, wanting to make sure it was clear, though I had no idea what the new Don Parks might look like. Clearly, he wouldn't look like the smug prick that'd been following me for weeks, which had tried to kill me and was now flowing towards the sewage treatment plant. The only thing I knew for sure was that he was still a man. That isn't always a guarantee.

"Go sit and I'll put the stuff in the trunk," I suggested to her. "It's getting chilly. No need for the little one there to freeze her butt off."

She did, and I made quick work of putting the stuff away. As I put my hands on the trunk to slam it shut, I heard a noise coming from behind and suspected the worst. In one fluid motion, I slammed the trunk down, slid my Tincher from my belt, and then spun around knowing I was about to be attacked. I imagined Parks had no doubt taken something from Godfrey, some ancient or alien artifact he'd wield with hopes of killing me, but when I turned, it was only two people, a young man and woman jogging past, not a care in the world. I hid the blade from sight, not wanting them to see it and freak out. I was sure they hadn't, as they both smiled and nodded as they moved by me, and continued on their way.

I let out a long breath and leaned against the car. I'd been so sure, so ready for something that my heart was pounding in my ears. Laughter was close to coming out when I went to get back in the car, but I saw someone standing in the road, less than thirty feet from the front end of the vehicle, a long shard of wood in his hand. I might not have known who it was, but the wood in his hand clearly had symbols carved in it, ones I knew to belong to Pharryn.

"Make this easier on yourself, Dillon. Come with me now, and I won't even look at that bitch twice. You make this hard, and she will suffer for every bit of pain and exertion you cause me to put out."

I took a slow step towards him. I reached my hand into my

pocket, ready to act. My fingers wrapped around the handle of the Tincher, and I started to take in long, deep breaths, ready for whatever the other hunter meant to throw my way. I had no intention of going anywhere with Parks. I wouldn't let him know that, though. I wanted him to think he was in control.

"Fine. You leave her alone, and I'll come with you," I lied and took a step forward. "But you have to promise me."

He laughed. "Would you believe my promise?"

"No. I'm not sure I would. So, why don't you let me give her the car keys and she can leave and it'll just be you and me." I took another step towards the front of the car, toward Parks.

"And why would I do that? Why would I give you anything you want?" he shouted, and I was starting to feel like a cowboy in some shootout at sundown.

"Because if you don't, I'll fight. I might lose in the end, but you might as well. It's a fifty-fifty thing here. But if you let her go now, allow her drive away from here, well, I won't fight at all. I'll drop my weapon and let you do what you're here to do."

"Dillon, no!" Rouge called out from inside the car. I turned and looked at her, giving her a bit of a smile, and a wink Parks wouldn't be able to see.

"I have to, Rouge. Things have a way of coming full circle, if you get me," I whispered with a nod I hoped she understood, before turning back to Parks in his new body. "Do we have a deal, or do I see how many times I can kill you before you stop coming back?"

Parks said nothing for a moment. I could see he was considering the idea, trying to figure out if there was some sort of trick happening, if I had some plan to make him look like the fool I already knew he was. I didn't really need a plan to do that. He was more than capable of making himself look like an utter jackass without any assistance from me.

"Fine. Give her the keys and then you lie down like the dog you are," Parks said, swinging the wood, looking ready to hit me with it.

I tossed the keys to her and listened as she started the car.

"Now, on the ground, Dillon."

"Not until she's gone." I turned back to look at Rouge one more time, mouthing that I loved her as she backed the car up, and drove off in the opposite direction to the hunter set on killing me, or at the very least, sending me back to the Collective. I watched as she drove up the street, turning left at the first intersection, and hoped I'd see her again soon.

"Okay. She's gone now, Dillon. We had a deal. On the ground," Parks shouted, and I smiled again to myself.

I turned and faced Parks again. I took my hands out of my pocket, leaving the Tincher where it was. I showed him empty hands, and a lie that I had no way to protect myself. I did make a deal with him, promised if he let her go I wouldn't put up a fight. I wanted him to feel as though I had no intention of doing anything at all, make him feel as safe and relaxed as I could. If he let his guard down enough, he wouldn't be ready when the strike happened.

"Get on the ground, Dillon. Now! We had a deal."

"Why are you doing this?" I asked, trying to buy some time, not ready to just bow out and hand myself over yet. There was still that tickle in the back of my head that Parks might be an agent of some other nefarious group, and not the Collective at all. I wanted to see if he would admit to it, or even slip up a little. I wanted to see the look on his face when I confronted him. "Are you really working for the Collective, or are you part of the problem, one of the bastards trying to bring it all down?"

"Bring it all down? What are you going on about? I work for the Collective, and they want you off Earth. One way or another."

He looked unfazed by the question. Not even a flicker; if anything, there was only a slight look of confusion.

"If you do work for the Collective, why do you have such a hard-on for me, for following the rules like this? Was what I did really so wrong?"

"Yes. It was," he said, sounding flabbergasted. He all but threw his hands up as if to say *check out this fucking guy*. "And I know, and the Collective knows, you won't stop breaking all the rules you can until you're made to stop. Now get on the ground, Dillon, or I'll make it worse than it has to be. Keep this up and I'll track down your gutter rat when we're done here."

"Watch what you say about her!" I yelled out, acting angrier than I was actually feeling. I knew he wouldn't be able to touch her. She was human, and the killing of a human in anything but the most self-defensive situation was the worst thing any hunter could do. "How much worse could you possibly make it for me, Parks? You want me to leave the place I've called home for more than twice as many years as I've been in this body to give up the first person I've ever loved, all because they say I broke a few rules? Look at everything I've managed to do here—in just the last few years alone I've stopped major disasters—but nothing is good enough, is it? And now here you are, loyal servant of the faceless, those who have no idea what it's like to be on a planet they weren't born on, alone, forced to protect humans, to defend the laws the Collective has made, and never make any sort of friends or connections. Could you do that?"

"I'm not here to debate with you, Dillon. I'm here to do a job. Same as you were. Now, let's finish this."

"You're so eager to end it. Do you hate this place that much?"

Parks shook his head, and even at that distance I could see his patience was wearing thin. I knew he wasn't going to wait too much longer before he simply charged at me, weapon swinging, but I wanted to keep him talking a little bit longer.

"I can see you don't want to answer that, but you seem to really want to get this over with without even hearing me out. Do you even know what I found in Niagara Falls?"

"I don't care."

"So you only care about the wrong I do, nothing about the good, is that it? You care enough to hunt me down without even slowing down to hear me out. If you and the Collective are so concerned with what I'm doing here, why don't you or the powers that be care about what I've achieved? Who and what I'm sending from this place is far worse than me and anything I'm doing. I'd like to see you do anything like this."

"I'm not a judge, Dillon. I'm not here to listen to your pleas, to try and understand your case. I'm here to send you back so they can hear your bullshit and decide what to do with you. But if you don't want to go away easy, then I will be your executioner, and that would give me more pleasure than you could possibly imagine. You and your human bitch killed me, or at least tried to. Do you know how it feels to blink out for that second, only to wake up in some strange body, in a strange place?"

"I do, but—"

"Well, I hadn't until I found you. Now, get on the ground, like I told you, and I will follow the orders given to me. If you keep wasting my time, I will kill your body and the true essence of you, since I've been told to rid Earth of you one way or another."

"I'm sorry you feel like I'm wasting your time," I told him, and was ready to end it. "I just need a moment."

"For what?"

"For her," I said as the engine of my car roared from behind Parks, seconds before the front end smashed him in the back. He didn't even get a chance to turn around and see it bearing down on him before the tires turned his new body into a bloody mess.

I'd hoped Rouge had gotten my meaning when I said that things come around full circle. Clearly she had.

She pulled the car up beside me and I hopped into the passenger's seat.

"How many times can I save you, Dillon?" she laughed nervously before driving off.

"Hopefully every time I need it," I told her as we drove off. "When he wakes up in another body, he is not going to be too pleased."

"What now?"

"We need to lay low. Very low, but first we need to go and check up on Godfrey."

His shop was a mess. The windows were smashed in; the lock on the door was ruined. I worried that when we entered, there would be something terrible waiting for us on the other side. I could tell Parks had a mean streak in him, knew he was not the type to just ask, and threaten, and the condition on Godfrey's shop proved that.

Tentatively, I opened the door and the two of us stepped in. I had my Tincher out the second we were out of sight of the main street, and once in there, I could see the inside was as bad as the outside. The display cases were smashed, relics ruined, and there were huge gouges in the walls where it looked as though someone—Parks of course—had taken a bat to them. At least there was no sign of blood, or Godfrey's body.

"You think he's okay?" Rouge whispered as we walked towards the back room where Godfrey kept his most treasured items.

"I hope so," I said, but I had little hope that he wouldn't be hurt in some way.

Stepping over the broken glass and something metal that had been twisted into a near-pretzel shape, we went through the curtains and moved into the back room. There was a terrible smell there, like kerosene and shit. I looked around to try and see what it was, thinking for a moment it might be the smell of Godfrey rotting, seeing as he wasn't human. I had no idea how his people smelled as they decomposed. I explained this to Rouge, telling her he might look human, but wasn't, though his situation wasn't the same as me or Parks. His appearance was an illusion, gone once he stepped out of the store.

"Are you sure you want to be here for this?" I asked her, nearly certain we were going to find his body.

"I think I need to be," she whispered, and we continued to search.

I looked everywhere out in the open, in the closets, and under the two tables there, but found no sign of him. There was little in that back room at all other than more broken displays, busted furniture, and holes in the wall. I'd been back here more than once, and took note that many of the items Godfrey normally stored here weren't destroyed like they were out front, they were missing. It was possible Parks took them all, but I held onto the hope that Godfrey had taken them and decided to disappear for a while.

After ten minutes or looking everywhere, even in the basement under the store, we found nothing.

"At least there's no blood. I'm holding onto that as a good sign," Rouge whispered, and we decided to leave. "Have you tried calling his cell?"

I shook my head. I hadn't thought of that at all. I figured Parks had taken Godfrey's phone when leaving after he called me. I thought this as it would explain why Godfrey hadn't called me afterwards. Still, there was no harm in trying to call it now. If Parks still had it, it was on his destroyed body, lying in the street by Rouge's house.

I dialed the number and hit send. As the phone rang in my ear, I could hear Godfrey's distinctive ringtone coming from somewhere in the store. The song playing was the theme from Star Trek Deep Space Nine. I let the phone ring and looked for it, sure that we were about to find his body, but instead, all we found was Godfrey's old-fashioned flip phone taped under a desk. As I removed it, the phone call ended and went to voicemail. As I hung it up, I heard something in the message and swore under my breath.

"What is it?" Rouge asked as I dialed the number back and let it ring through. I put it on speaker phone so she could hear it too.

"Dillon, if you hear this, I'm going underground. That hunter is a madman, and I won't be safe if I stay here. Keep your phone close. I'll call you when I can."

"At least he left you something and you know he's alive."

I nodded and hoped he really was. There was something slightly paranoid in my head that made me worry the phone and the message had been planted by Parks, but I had to hold onto the idea that Godfrey was fine and had gone into hiding. The problem was the strange smell in the room, the source of which we never found.

"We should get out of here," I finally said, and headed back towards the front door.

"Any idea of where to go?"

"No, but we'll figure it out."

Our first stop was to the carwash to get the bits of blood off the hood and grille left on it when Rouge pulverized Parks. It wasn't nearly as messy as I was expecting, and after an hour, we were done and back on the road. The next stop was to a car dealership in Scarborough, a place called the *Loan Arranger* on Kingston Road. Parks knew what my car looked like, so I was hoping to trade it in and prepared to pay a little extra for something he wouldn't know was mine. I got way less than I had paid for it, but money wasn't something I cared about that much. I was leaning towards a Dodge Charger, but Rouge said she always wanted a Jeep, and there just happened to be an olive-green Jeep Wrangler available.

"And that colour green would so go with my red hair," she chuckled, and did a pinup girl pose against it, so I was sold. It was a big vehicle, not like the old Jeeps, and there was a little voice in the back of my head that thought It may stick out like a sore thumb. Then again, how many Jeeps did I see on the streets these days? More than a dozen, that was for sure.

After we paid for the Jeep and signed all the paperwork, we drove across town to Sue's house. Sue was Rouge's friend, the one who would usually dog-sit for us when needed. Rouge called her ahead of time to make sure it would be okay, and of course she was more than happy to. She called the little one her spirit animal, and told us to take as long as we needed before we came to pick her back up.

We drove off, Rouge sad at having to leave her baby again so soon. We'd only picked her the day before, after we both went off to finish a case in Niagara Falls, and already we were leaving her again.

"She's going to think I don't love her," Rouge said, her voice quiet and sad as we drove to a motel on Lakeshore.

"That's not true. You'll always be her mom. It's just not safe for her to be running around with us right now. You know that."

"I do, but it doesn't make it any easier."

"Nothing about this is easy."

Sunday/Monday/Tuesday

The next three days were slow and felt like copies of one another. I kept my phone close, in case Godfrey called, but left the ringer on silent, just in case. I had no idea how crafty Parks might be. I knew he wouldn't have the resources to track my phone like I would his—if I even knew his number. He was new here, hadn't made friends with any police officers, and that made things easier. It was one less thing to worry about.

Each night we moved to a different motel; most of them were only a small step away from being little more than a crackhouse. There was always a smell lingering in the air, on the carpets, and the wood or veneer surfaces had a film or stickiness to them. Each one was different, yet they were clearly odour relatives. On the first night I went and grabbed our own sleeping bags to use, and picked up a few packs of those antibacterial wipes. I did anything to help make sleeping a little less funky.

For those three days we spent our time trying to come up with a plan, a way to catch and eventually kill Parks. In the first room, I dumped out my bag and went through everything in it to see exactly what I might be able to use to do the job. I was pretty sure my Tincher wouldn't work on him, but I did have a few other things that might do the trick. To be honest, when I checked what I had, I put most of my chips on something in a metal bottle called Refulgent. It is basically a brilliant light, something taken from the heart of a fire demon that will blind and eventually devour whoever you set it upon. I was pretty sure it would kill anything, body and spirit. Even me.

I would have to be a little careful with that one, if I decided to use it.

"I'm just not sure how we're going to get him, or even where to start looking," Rouge said just as there was a knock on the door. My stomach grumbled at the food I knew was on the other side.

I opened the door, paid for our pizza and wings, and then sat down beside her.

"He knows my phone number. Eventually, we'll get a call from him and everything will come together."

"And if he doesn't?"

I shrugged and bit into a slice of cheesy goodness. "He's a hunter. Even if he doesn't do the obvious, all we have to do is bait a trap that will be impossible for him to stay away from. He fancies himself smart and clever, but he's never met the likes of me before." I gave her a wink and a smile as I hamster-cheeked a wad of chewed up food. I'm a charmer.

"More like he's never met the woman who keeps pulling your ass out of the fire."

I laughed at that and had to agree. "At least it's a nice ass, I hope."

I've always done this job as a lone wolf, but since meeting Rouge, she'd kept me from getting my clock punched more than once. So, even if Parks could figure me out, there was no way he was prepared for the likes of her. At least, that was my hope. In a way, Rouge was becoming the ace up my sleeve in all of this.

That night, she fell asleep, but I couldn't get my brain to shut off. I lay beside her, listened as her breathing slowed and her eyes began to flicker behind her lids. She looked so peaceful, so beautiful. It was one of the first moments I had to just stop and appreciate things. There was a time, not all that long ago, when I used to read books, nap while the sun was still up, and watch movies; days where I would waste time just walking through the park for fun. Yet, since the incident in Innisville with the Hellion, and everything that happened since, I hadn't had very much time to just take it easy and relax.

I reached out and touched her cheek and wondered how crazy

all this must be for her. Here she was, a woman who'd grown up with a normal life, went to school, worked as a salesperson for a while, had dreams of being a fashion designer in high school, and then turned into a burlesque queen. Now, she'd given all that up to join her boyfriend, someone not even from this planet, in hunting down monsters, demons, and spirits, putting her life on the line, and in turn was being hunted down along with me. And she could just shut it all down, close her eyes and sleep so easily. What an amazing person.

Quietly, I stepped out of bed and walked over to the window. I peeked out the curtain, careful not to open it too much and disturb her. I looked out at the world beyond. There was an obvious prostitute standing near the driveway, doing her best to lure people into her palace of pleasure. Two men who appeared more than a little tipsy were out there talking about the Leafs and drinking cheap beer, while a couple getting out of their car took each other's hands and headed off to a room. Life was moving on without a care in the world. None of them knew what was going on outside their own little lives, the bizarre world of monsters and creatures desperate to force their way in. How many of them witnessed evidence of monsters, or things from beyond, and blew it off to the wind, the shadows playing games with their heads, or just blamed it on a little too much to drink?

I know it's easier for people to just brush those things off. It was simpler for someone to think their mind was having a go at them, that they were a bit too tired or overworked, than it was to believe things existed outside the realm of normality. People who met me would think I was mad if I just told them even though I look human, I was one of the last of a slaughtered race of aliens millions of lightyears away from here. When I told Rouge about it, she took it better than I expected. I had never disclosed it to anyone I'd known for that short a period of time, and she heard it and took it so well. I'm not sure others would, nor would they think: *Well, there's someone I will start to date, now that I know he's an alien*. I still haven't told her exactly how old I am, which could be another thing she would freak out about.

I closed the curtain and went over to the single chair in the room and sat in the dark, eyes going back over to the bed where Rouge was sleeping. I tried not to be envious as I did, and instead went through the ways things might go for us, and for Parks. I didn't want to tell her my true fear when it came to him and the Collective. Partly that was because saying it out loud made it real, and making it real meant I might have to actually act on it. In the dark, alone with the sounds of her slow, steady breath, the muffled noises out beyond our room, and my own thoughts, it was harder to get away from.

There was a good chance we'd be able to kill Parks once and for all, get him off our backs, but then what? If the Collective had really sent him, and he wasn't some agent of a group set to destroy the laws protecting Earth, then what would stop them from sending another hunter after us? How many would they send after me before they either gave up, or killed me, maybe hurting or killing Rouge in the process? It was something I needed to think about, but I didn't want to. The threat was there, making my nerves twitch, because if they sent more and more hunters after me, eventually I would die, or I'd be on the run for the rest of my life. Would Rouge join me in that? Would she be okay not just leaving Toronto, but never calling anywhere home for very long?

This made sleep even harder for me, and I sat there for a long time before I drifted off.

I woke up the next day sore and stiff in the chair, my muscles filled with cramps and my mind with regrets. I couldn't stifle the old-man groaning as I stood up, and that woke Rouge from what appeared to be the best sleep ever. She sat up, hair little more than tousled, smiling and looking as though she had already been awake, eaten, and put on make-up.

Must.

Be.

Nice.

"You sleep well?" she asked, probably not knowing I'd been in the chair all night.

"As well as I could," I said, keeping my slumber vessel a secret. "You look as though you caught up. Gorgeous as ever."

"I love the compliments, sweet man, but I would love a tea even more. You want to wait for me to get ready, or would you be a dear and score us some caffeine while I wash this motel off of me?"

I smiled and agreed to go for a breakfast run.

I locked the door and headed out to the car, forgetting for a moment that I was now a Jeep owner. There was a split second when panic set in, as I was sure someone had stolen my car. An act I wouldn't put past the area we were in.

But there it was. An olive-green monster that looked more ready for some mountains than it did for the very flat landscape of the city. I hopped in, turned on the heat, and drove away from the motel. I hooked my phone up to the stereo and put on some CCR to keep me company, since it's the best music for driving in my opinion, and checked where the closest *Tim Horton's* was. My phone gave me directions, and I was off.

I was nearly halfway there when I wondered if the two of us should start thinking about some sort of disguise. I mean, something as simple as a hat and sunglasses would work for me in a pinch, but Rouge might need one that was a little better. She has a very eye-catching look, from the red hair, the alabaster skin, and the shape of her very shapely body. She could turn heads even when she was wearing a hoodie and jeans, so it might be easier to stay out of sight if we lowered our visibility.

I would talk to Rouge about it when I got back to the room, maybe even suggest she dye her hair, though that might be pushing things a little too far.

There was no drive-thru at the *Tim Hortons* closest to us, so I parked out front, and went into the tiny store to place my order. There was the usual smell in there of coffee and baked goods, but there was another one I knew all too well. It was the smell of stale cigarettes and unwashed body, but with a hint of something worse, and familiar. I couldn't put my finger on the last part so I looked around to find the source, an act that didn't take long as there were only two tables, and a row of six stools by the window.

There were two teenagers on the stools, and at one of the tables was a person hunched over, wearing layer after layer of ragged coats and blankets, paint-stained pants, and shoes that appeared to be made out of duct tape. I assumed that was the source of the rankness, and was surprised the employees allowed someone who smelled like that to stay there, especially with so many people coming in and out for food. But it's a different time now. People have become too scared to say things for their own safety, and because they don't want to look insensitive. You never know when someone is filming you, waiting for a perfect moment to put you up on YouTube or some other social media platform. I can't blame them for that. I know exactly what that feels like.

I placed my order; two bagels, two cookies, a tea, and coffee, before I headed back out. When I turned around to leave, I noticed the homeless man or woman was gone, but the smell lingered on. I held my breath and passed the spot where the cloud of stench hung. I took in a deep gasp of air as soon as I stepped out into the fresh air. I closed my eyes, turned my head towards the early morning sun, before heading back to the Jeep. I wasn't more than two steps away from the door, when I heard someone call my name, and my empty stomach turned cold and dropped deep down into my gut. The food and drinks nearly slipped from my hands.

I had nothing on me. No Tincher, no dagger, and no gloves. All I had brought was my wallet because I was sure I would just use a drive-thru and be on my way. My name was called again, and cautiously I turned to the left, to the source. I prepared myself to toss what I had just bought and run if need be. If it was Parks in a new body, or some creature who knew who I was, there would be little I could do to stop them.

"Don't be such a baby, Dillon. It's me," the strange voice said, and when I turned around, it was the homeless person I'd seen inside Tim Hortons. They were still buried under layers of dirty coats and blankets, but I for the first time I could see their face and knew who it was right away.

"Godfrey?" I said, staring at the face of something closer to a crocodile or lizard than the person I knew in the shop. It was his real face. I had never heard him whisper before, and the accent almost all but disappeared when he did.

"Oh, aren't you the smart one today? Did my good looks give it away?"

"Why are you dressed like that?" I asked, looking him up and down and catching another whiff of his very strong, terrible odour. Some of it was what I had smelled back in his shop.

"Oh, you think I should be wearing some nice slacks and maybe a nice dress shirt, do you? Or maybe a leather jacket, a hoodie, and some jeans, so we can look like twins?" he said with clear anger in his voice as I moved closer to him to make sure there were less eyes on us. "I look like this because dressing like a homeless person is the one sure way to ensure people don't really notice me. Sure, they'll see me, but then they do everything they can to pretend as though I'm not there at all. Especially when I'm carrying around some old garbage I found at the back of the grocery store down the street. Even if I was bleeding on the ground, people in this city would just walk over me rather than actually acknowledge me."

I nodded and gave him another look. "Well, you really are selling it."

"I have to. That bastard is after you, and wants to make my life hell until he gets you."

"I'm sorry he went after you," I told him with all the sincerity I could offer. I had no idea the extent of which Parks had gone after him, whether he hurt him or not, but I had seen the condition of the shop; from the sheer fact that he was out here, dressed like that, on the run, I knew it was bad.

"It could have been worse, I guess, but the little prick destroyed so much of my shop, stole a few things, and threatened me with my own weapons."

"I know. We stopped by your shop. I should've known you were in there from that smell. What is it?"

"Oh, that! I had a bottle of Hyrio piss and Parks smashed it. It's strong and almost impossible to wash off. But do you know how rare it is? He really is a turd blossom."

I agreed with him, though I had no idea just how hard it was to get that type of urine. Not really one of the things I specialize in. "How did you know to wait for me here?"

"I had no idea you would come here," he told me, and shifted some of his layers. "I was just hanging out here, enjoying the people talking and the smells. Plus, there's free Wi-Fi in there, and I've been downloading stuff onto my tablet," he chuckled, and showed me the iPad he had hidden in one of his coats. "I'm not doing anything these days, can't meet with contacts or hunters, so it's all about binge watching shows. Have you seen Peaky Blinders? So good."

I hadn't, but it was on my watch list once things in my life settled down a bit, or maybe while we were hiding out from Parks in some of the hotels.

"So, I guess it's just good luck that we ran into each other," I said, and he shook his head.

"Good luck? How do you know Parks doesn't already know where you are? How do you know he doesn't have little trolls of his own combing the streets for you? He no doubt does, and now they'll know where I am, too."

"I don't know for sure, but I'm doing my best to cover my tracks. Rouge already killed him again."

"Again? She did the first one, too?" I nodded and he laughed. "That woman makes one damn fine hunter. Have you finally agreed to let her work with you, or are you still being a stubborn bastard about it?"

"She was determined, so it was either work together, or work together. I chose to work together."

"Good man. Where is she now?"

"We're shacked up in a hotel trying to figure out our next move."

"Your next move should be getting out of Toronto. You two should just disappear, go and be happy with one another. The Collective and Parks have no idea where you might choose to hide, and if you take the cash you have, move to some little farm out in the middle of nowhere, how would they ever find you?"

Godfrey's idea was sound, one I hadn't fully thought of, though there had been an inkling of an idea there. But as he said it, I had no idea why it hadn't been my first thought. I should've just packed up, headed out to the middle of nowhere, bought a yurt and lived like a hermit.

"What about you?" I asked Godfrey and shot a look over my shoulder, just to be safe and make sure nobody was paying much attention to us. "Do you want to come with us?"

Godfrey shook his head and let out a little laugh. "I'm not one for the country life. Too quiet. I love the noise of the city. Not to mention the fact that I have a prison term here, and eventually, I want to actually go home, see my family. With what Parks did to my shop, I'm sure the Collective won't blame me for leaving. I can easily say that I didn't want to try and explain to the police about the damage. Can you imagine what would happen if they ask me to come down to the station? I think I'm good and covered, Dillon. It's you and your lady who need to get going. But if you need anything, you know how to get a hold of me."

"I do?" I said. "Isn't your phone still at the shop?"

"Well, you'll know how to get a hold of me when things blow over, then."

"Good enough for me," I said and began to laugh.

"What's so funny?"

"You. Us. For so many years, I considered you quite a bastard. You sold me shitty goods so many times, nearly got me killed a few more, and now here we are, and I consider you one the only real friends I have. How sad is that?"

"The sentiment is mutual; all of them, including you being a bit of a bastard."

"You know, I'd hug you or something, but you smell like a sewer rat that has bathed in a dead body, and like you said, it's not easy to wash off."

"Well, you smell like a cheap motel, and human. Just as nasty, if you ask me."

"To each their own. At least a long hot shower will fix this," I said, and before I left, I had one more question for him: "Did you manage to save any of your items, or did Parks get them all?"

"I managed to grab a few things. I wasn't going to let him clean me out. He had no idea where to look, the shit!"

"Well, I hope I won't need anything else, but I'm glad you've got something, because you never know, right? Even though I plan on getting out of here in the next few days, better to have all bases covered. Just in case."

"So he's okay?" Rouge asked after I got back to the motel and told her about my impromptu meeting with Godfrey.

"As well as can be, but I'm glad to see he got out in one piece."

"What's he doing now? Why didn't you bring him here?"

I explained to her everything that had been said between us, mainly the talk of moving out into the sticks, while he stayed in the city to ensure the Collective didn't punish him even more. She thought it was a good plan, on all sides. The only question now is, when do we leave?

"I think the sooner the better," I told her, looking around the room. "We can pack up what we have, and just drive in one direction or another, until we decide to stop. Would you be okay with that? Leaving the city and all?"

She was silent for a moment, and I worried she would say no. This was not her fight really, not her battle, despite the fact that she was the one who'd killed Parks twice. She had a life here, friends, a whole community of burlesquers who she talked to on the regular, despite having giving up dancing herself. She'd grown up in Toronto, lived surrounded by the high rises, city noise, and an ocean of people. Now I was asking her to turn in a completely opposite direction, asking her to move out into the middle of nowhere, where she would have no friends, no family. She'd be a stranger in a strange land, something I could easily relate to.

"When do we leave?" she said with a smile, breaking the silence and filling me with relief.

"You're sure?"

"As sure as I want to finish this food and then see if we can make this room a little dirtier," she said with a wink, and sipped her tea. I would like to see that too.

Wednesday

We were packed early the next day, ready to start our road trip, drive to our new and much quieter life. Rouge had already called Sue and told her she would stop by later in the day to pick up the pup. The sky was grey beyond the room, but our moods were bright. I was more than a little excited at the idea of the journey we were about to embark on. As far as I could tell, Rouge was too.

Rouge went to the car to warm it up while I headed over to the front desk to pay everything off. Rouge told me to hurry, that she wanted to see her little fur beast as soon as possible. I walked into the front office, the place reeking of cheap cigarettes and stale sweat, and I wanted to hurry for my own reasons. I walked over to the desk, waited for a moment before I rang the bell.

I waited a few seconds more, and rang it again when there was no response.

Then again.

And again.

On the fifth time, a tired looking man who was the very stereotype of what you would expect a shady motel worker would look like sauntered out; complete with stained bathrobe that looked as though it was made from a couch circa 1970. He walked out slowly, scratching his ample belly and yawning.

"What?" he grumbled, looking as though I was some sort of inconvenience to him.

"I want to pay for my room, to check out," I told him, and he groaned.

"Fine. Cash or credit?"

I said nothing but handed over my credit card and waited for him to finish the transaction. As he was trying to figure out the intricacies of the credit/debit machine, I turned around and scanned the small, dirty office. My eyes were immediately drawn to a copy of the *Toronto Sun*. I couldn't help but notice it, thanks to their typical flashy front page where I saw a photo of someone I knew. I walked over, reading the headline as I did.

'Eighth Headless Body Baffles Police'

And there, under the headline among the photos of what appeared to be the victims, was a picture of Detective Garcia. He looked more stressed than I'd ever seen him, and I wondered if this had anything to do with what he'd called me for the other day. I picked up the paper, and skimmed through the brief article. It told a horrible tale. Since the previous Friday, the bodies of eight men had been found in motels, alleys, and vehicles; foul play was clear as all of them were missing their heads. There had been no word on any suspects or motive from police, but the way the reporter made it sound, it was as though the investigators were just fools bumbling around the crime scenes without a clue. I knew Garcia well enough to know he was nobody's fool. If he wasn't telling the media details, there was a reason for it, and it would have nothing to do with ineptitude.

"Here's your card, buddy. You want your continental breakfast?" the clerk said from behind me. I shook my head. I couldn't imagine a place like this offering any sort of food I'd want to put it in my stomach. I took my credit card and the newspaper and headed out to the Jeep and Rouge.

"That took a while," she said as I stepped in. I tossed the paper on her lap. "What's this?" I watched her as she read the headline and skimmed the article. "What the fuck is going on in this city?"

"I don't know, but I think this was why Garcia was calling me the other day. He said something strange was going with a case and wanted me to look at it. But I was too busy and I never thought to call him back. Shit!" I tried not to feel bad about it, but seeing the look on Garcia's face, it made it harder to swallow the cold feeling I had in my chest.

"It's not your fault, Dillon. Things have been nuts. You don't even know if this is something in your wheelhouse anyway."

"I know, but what if it is? What if this *is* something I could've helped Garcia with, but because of all this mess with Parks, I didn't do anything?" I said, and was more than a little pissed off. If none of this crap had been going on with Parks and the Collective hunting me down, I would have been able to be there for Garcia. It might have come to nothing, but then again, if this was something from off-world, I might've been able to help and even stop any further deaths.

"Now what?" Rouge asked as we sat in the running Jeep. I looked out the window, at the road that would lead us out of the city into hiding, but I found my eyes going back to the cover of the newspaper.

"Well, what would you do? This is your life now too, so what do we do? Run or try and help?"

Rouge stared down at the newspaper for less than five seconds, and then pulled out her phone. "Let me call Sue and tell her we aren't coming right away. You should probably call Garcia."

I pulled up to Garcia's house ten minutes after getting off the phone with him. He was already in his driveway, looking as dishevelled as he had on the front page of the newspaper.

"Nice car," he said, and stepped into the back seat. "It's fancier inside than I was expecting. Your last car looked like something you'd expect to be towed off to a scrap yard, or used in a crash derby."

"And how are you, Detective?" I said sarcastically. "Sorry about everything going to shit, and me not calling sooner. Things have been a mess." I gave him a quick rundown of everything that had happened with the Niagara Falls case, my stopover in a mental hospital, and Parks, of course.

"That's the guy you had us arrest?" he asked, and I nodded. "It's no wonder you were so stressed when I called on Saturday."

"You don't know the half of it," Rouge said, and I nudged her. I was okay with Garcia knowing about a lot of what it was

I did, but I really didn't want him to know about disposing of Parks' body in the tub, or running him down. Those details were left out of the story I told him. He was still a police officer, after all, and although he had seen his fair share of weird, some of the ideas of what we deal with might be hard for him to wrap his head around.

"How so?" Garcia asked, and I just chuckled and shook my head.

"You know how it is, Garcia," I tried to deflect. "The things I do and the things I see, there's just so much craziness. Well, enough about us, what about the case?"

"Is it okay to do this with both of you here?" he asked, motioning towards Rouge. "No offense. I'm not saying that because you're a woman or anything. More like, I don't know how much you know of what Dillon does."

"She knows more than you, to be honest, so yeah, she's good," I said, and smiled at Rouge, who clearly wasn't taking any offense to the remark.

"Well, these things are pretty graphic too. I've warned everyone I've shown them to since this started. This is not your average homicide case."

"Thanks for the heads-up," Rouge nodded, and looked as though she was ready for anything he might show. "We want to help with the case if we can."

"There's not much of a case right now, other than all the bodies." Garcia reached into his briefcase and pulled out a file folder. "On Friday I was called out to a Holiday Inn near West Mall and Permfield Path. The cleaner went in and found a man there with his head missing. The victim was Harold Kane, a businessman from New York who was in town for a meeting with some other business types. He was last seen on camera leaving the hotel at ten at night, and there is no sign of him returning, but his body was found in the room, naked, and headless. You think this has anything to do with the headless guy in Niagara Falls?"

He handed me a photo of the corpse. Rouge took one look, made a gurgling sound and turned her head. I couldn't blame her. There was a part of me that wanted to do the same. The picture was very graphic, bloody, and he was very naked, but the wound was nothing like that of Chance's, the real estate agent and developer from Niagara Falls. *His* head had been twisted of, charred around the edges. This photo showed the wound to be smooth and clean, not to mention very bloody. There was no twist action here at all. I had no idea what I was looking at.

"There was no sign of a weapon used, no blade or saw marks on the skin or spinal cord. In fact, the spinal cord appears to have been snapped, not cut. Which, in case either of you don't know, is not an easy thing."

I handed him back the photo and agreed. Even breaking someone's neck isn't as easy as it seems in the movies. Once, many years back when I was down in the United States where I was first assigned, I had been attacked by a group of criminals. They were all armed with guns, and a demon from the Shia'zz species. I was sure I was going to die, and to save myself I tried to break the neck of one of the men. It seemed simple enough. At the time, movies were not a thing, but I had seen farmers do it to chickens. I gave it my best shot, squeezing and twisting the man's head, but all it did was pull a muscle in his neck and piss him off. Luckily, he dropped his gun in the struggle and I managed to pick it up and shoot him in the leg so I could get away. It's strange to remember that story now, and a few others from the same period where I hurt or even killed a human and never got in any trouble for it. Well, it was a different time back then, and the rules weren't nearly as strict as they are now.

"The reason I called you was what we found on this body, and the second one we found the next day." He handed me another photo. This one was taken from inside a car. The man was leaned back in the front driver's seat, pants and underwear down to his ankles, the dress shirt he wore soaked red with the blood from his open neck. "We found some strange substances on the wounds of the victim. I called you when the samples from the first came back, while I was with the second victim and saw more of it there. Same stuff has been found on all eight bodies." He passed over a medical report with a bunch of words that were too long and made no sense to me at all.

"Do you have a version of that report that is suitable for people who enjoy reading more Charlene Harris, less Clive Barker?"

"Basically there's an unknown substance, and some form of silicone mixed with it."

"Silicone?" Rouge asked, coming back to the conversation after taking a breather.

"Yeah. The silicone is the same type used for hundreds of different things, pink in colour, but I think it's the unknown substance that makes this more of a case for Dillon than just me," Garcia said, and offered more of the photos of the other crime scenes. I put up my hand and asked if there was anything in them that would help with the case, not really wanting to see more dead bodies than I had to. "They're all pretty much the same. Same wounds, very bloody, all in some form of nudity; meaning either naked or pants down."

"Suggesting they all were engaged in some sort of sexual activity," Rouge jumped in before I had the chance. I'm sure I would have thought of that too, but I was still focused on the missing heads.

"Each of them had recently ejaculated. No condoms used, and no signs of DNA other than their own. The M.E. did find trace amounts of silicone there as well, but none of the foreign substance. Does that tell you anything, Dillon? Rouge?"

We both shook our heads.

"Is there anything the victims have in common?" Rouge asked, and it was a better question than I was thinking. I was going to ask Garcia if any of them smelled weird, thinking that maybe an odour would help give away if this had anything to do with something not of Earth.

"Not really. Victims one, seven, and eight were all business people. Victims three and four were university students. Victim five worked in a factory, and victim six was a retired cop. All different ages, multiple races, and only two of them had minor criminal records. There is nothing even remotely linking any of these people together, and they were murdered all over the city—west, east and central, mainly—so we're all just banging our heads against the wall. The fact that they are happening one after another—three of them were found on Sunday alone—everyone is having a fit to find out who, or in my case *what*, is doing this. You have to have some idea, right?"

I didn't. There wasn't enough to go on, other than some really graphic photos and some very weird circumstances. I was about to tell him that when his phone went off, and he told me to hold on a second.

"Garcia," he said when he answered it. "Yeah. Where? I'll be there in less than twenty." He hung up and sat back hard in the Jeep. "You want to see one of these scenes firsthand?"

"There was another one?" I asked, not sure if I did want to be there to witness it, but I knew if there were any details to notice, things the cops would overlook like unusual smells, then I really should be there.

"Yeah. Down by Mimico and Lakeshore. Guy was found behind a building, naked, and his head missing."

"You up for this?" I asked Rouge.

She shrugged. "Is anyone ready for something like this?"

"Never," Garcia said, and he told me where to go.

We pulled up to the scene. Police cars and other emergency vehicles lined the street. There was no media yet, but I had no doubt they would be there soon. This was a huge case, an ongoing series of murders that would get a ton of coverage. The media loved to lead with blood and death, the more gruesome the better. From what I already knew about the case, this was probably making the newspaper editors and newscast producers drool. After all, this would be victim number nine in six days.

Garcia asked us to wait in the car for a moment, while he went out and spoke to whoever he needed to in order to get us past the police tape. In a way, it was a good thing we were in hiding. We were both dressed down, not really in disguise, but also not looking very eye-catching—normally more a problem for Rouge than me, of course.

"So, does this mean we're not leaving any time soon?" Rouge asked from the passenger seat when we were alone.

I shook my head, not really sure how to answer the question. I was pretty sure we should. I knew it would be easier to pack up and run, getting lost in the wilderness of Canada, but there was still something in me that felt a call to help. I had a sense of duty to help Garcia and to do what I always do, especially if this was something otherworldly. If there was something off-planet here killing people—which might not be the case—I didn't think I would be able to run off and leave this in the hands of Garcia; even if deep down it was exactly what I wanted to do.

"We'll see what's going on here first," I told her. "If there's something I can do to help, I will, but we'll still lay low until we can get out of the city."

"Yay! More sketchy motels," she laughed, but there was little humour in her voice. "We should invest in hand sanitizer and anti-bacterial wipes if we're going to stay in these motels much longer."

"I know. Maybe we can find somewhere a little less motel, a little more—"

"Clean?"

"Yeah. Clean." Rouge pointed out the window when she saw Garcia was coming back to the car, his face as hard to read as something in a foreign language I'd never learned.

"Okay, we're good to go," Garcia said, as he opened the door for us. "But if and when the media shows up, you two make yourself scarce. Last thing I want is to try to explain what you're doing here; especially with all the popularity you're experiencing because of that YouTube video."

I agreed, and we headed towards the police tape. I looked around, taking in the surrounding area as we went. I'd never been to this park before; I wasn't someone who liked to frequent Scarborough very often unless I had a case. I never had many of them: even monsters and demons stay away from there.

I'd heard stories about Morningside Park though, especially how it gets a night. The stories go, when the sun goes down, the place turns into a hookup spot. People park cars and have a go at it, others take to the bush and benches. In the '80s and '90s, when homosexuality was still not something you could be as open about, many men who were living secret lives would do so there.

We walked down the driveway, and then were led to a path where more uniformed officers stood around the public washrooms. Garcia told us the body was in there, already photographed and printed, waiting for us and the coroner to show up. We passed by the uniforms, felt their eyes on us, and Garcia told them all to wait outside while we went in.

There was a smell in there. It was the first thing I noticed. It was strong and coppery, which had to be the blood we would undoubtedly see, and old urine, which wasn't unusual in places like this. Garcia pointed over to the stalls, and I walked over to them with Rouge at my side.

"Wow," she whispered close to my ear. "That is some kind of smell."

I agreed and when we opened the stall door, we saw the source of the blood smell. There was a man sitting on the toilet with his pants around his ankles, flaccid penis stuck to the side of his leg, and his upper body soaked in blood. It had pooled under him too, around the base of the toilet, thick and gelatin-like. My eyes went to where the man's head once had been, and I wondered what he'd looked like before getting shorter. Judging by the colour of his pubic, arm and chest hair, I assumed he was older than the last victim.

Rouge made a strange sound, as though she was going to throw up, and then turned away from the scene, but didn't walk away.

"You okay?" I asked her, reaching over and putting my hand on her arm.

"Just need a second. Boy oh boy. Movies just never really capture what death looks like, do they? Or smells like."

"No they don't," I said, and looked closely at the scene in front of me.

There wasn't much to see. There was a partially nude man, sitting on a toilet with his head missing, blood all around him, and some strange, foamy liquid around the open neck. There seemed to be no footprints anywhere, no obvious signs of anyone else being in the stall with him, other than the missing head. Forensics might be able to find something else—random hairs and fingerprints—but this was a public bathroom, so I doubted there'd be anything viable, so I had to hope I'd manage to figure something out.

Rouge turned back and looked in the stall. She made another low, gagging sound. She grabbed hold of my shoulder, gripped it so hard it made me wince, and I could tell she was trying to steady herself.

"You don't have to be here for this part," I told her, and she gave me a look as though she could do it. It was her brave face, even though she looked paler than normal. "I mean it. You don't have to do this part of it, especially since this isn't the norm."

"No. I can manage. I can do this if you can," she said softly, and turned her attention to the body. "Are we looking for something specific?"

I didn't know what I was looking for. The main thing was to try and find something that didn't belong. A little piece of a bigger puzzle that might let me know one way or another if the killer was a monster from beyond the stars, or one that was human. Human monsters weren't what I dealt with, so in a way, I was crossing my fingers for that. This kind of violence was not something I enjoyed dealing with. I'd rather leave this to the earthbound police than have to get much more involved with something capable of this kind of carnage.

With how things had been going, though, I was sure I would find something to prove it was going to be in my realm of business. Aren't I the lucky one?

"Can I move in and get a closer look?" I asked Garcia, who nodded and told me all the photos and major evidence gathering had been done. That was good and bad. I would've preferred to see this place untouched, to note anything the police might've taken as evidence, but I would ask Garcia for photos later. I just preferred a fresh scene, unsullied.

I moved in, Rouge staying mainly at the stall door. She might've followed if she could, but there wasn't a whole lot of room in there. It wasn't a disability stall, after all. I could feel blood squish under my shoe, and the tile underneath made for a slippery surface. I had to be careful or I'd do a comical dance before falling over into blood Jell-O.

The copper in the air was thick, but I wanted to get a close up look at the wound. I grabbed the collar of my t-shirt and pulled it over my nose so as not to breathe any more of it in than I had to, and put my face within inches of the severed neck.

It was so strange. I've seen people with their heads cut off before. Once it was by a saw, another time it was from a sheet of metal; and of course there was Chance, but this was so different. The pictures only showed so much, but up close, you could really see there was no sign of how this was done. The wound was smoother than it was jagged, wet around the edges with blood and that foam I'd seen in the crime scene photos. I took a pen from my pocket and touched it, expecting it to sizzle, thinking maybe the head was melted off, but nothing happened. I pulled my pen away and there was a small, mucus tail dangling from it that told me nothing. I gave it a sniff, and it was close to scentless, though there was a hint of something, a thing you might smell on a summer breeze, though I couldn't quite put my finger on what it was exactly. I shook the slime off, reluctantly tucked the pen back into my jacket, and continued to look.

There was nothing else to really see. No bruising. No scratches or cuts anywhere else.

"Was anything major found that they might've already checked into evidence?" I asked, looking into the wound and seeing another snapped spinal cord.

"Nothing much," Garcia said, and looked at a sheet of paper which I assumed was the inventory. "Some random hairs, four cigarette butts which were from four different brands, a lighter, and some more silicone found in the wound. That's pretty much it."

So, nothing at all, I thought, and told him thanks. There was nothing here to suggest a monster or demon did this. Then again, there wasn't any clue that a human could've done it either. Sure, the weird foam and silicone were strange, but that didn't help to shine a light onto what could possibly be doing this. I was pretty sure there was no real help I could offer him until something else came up that would offer up some sort of lead to whoever was stealing these people's heads, so going on the run looked as though it was still on the table.

With that thought, I turned to leave, but when I did, I lost my balance in the pool of dark crimson. Determined not to make a splashdown, I struggled to regain my balance, swung my arms wildly, and eventually grabbed the top of each side of the stall to steady myself. I knew I must've looked hilarious, and I might've laughed too once I'd steadied my feet, but my clumsiness helped me find something I wouldn't have noticed if not for my rubber legs.

"What? What is it?" Rouge asked, clearly reading the look on my face.

I grasped it, and brought it down in front of me, not sure what it was from touch alone. When my hand grabbed the top of the stall wall, I'd noticed it was rough there, and worried I would cut myself. Then, I felt something soft and slightly cold. I nearly screamed at that, assuming it was a bug, and I hate insects, but I was quick to realize it was nothing alive. When I looked down at it I was horrified, though. It was a human finger, possibly a woman's as there was a long, red painted fingernail attached to it. I almost drop it to the floor in a moment of disgust, but stopped myself, and turned it over in my hand. It didn't take long to deduce it wasn't human, though, as there was no blood at the end of the severed digit, and nor was there any bone.

"Is that a finger?" Garcia asked from Rouge's side.

"It is, but it's not from him, or anyone else. It's made of rubber," I said, and held it out to him.

"Rubber, or silicone?" Rouge asked, making me feel dumb.

"I think you're right," I told her, and stepped out of the stall. "You know what that means?"

"We're not going anywhere," she replied, and I reluctantly nodded. Something was going on here, and I was more certain at that point it had nothing to do with anything natural.

We left shortly thereafter, having to sneak out a different way and be cautious getting back to our car. Garcia was called and told that the media had arrived, and they were anxious to get close to the restrooms. I had no plans on being featured on CP24, or CTV, so we cut through the woods, swinging around the far way, and getting back to the Jeep. I asked Garcia if he was staying or coming with us, and he shrugged.

"Do you think the finger means this is, you know, alien?" Garcia asked as we tramped through the woods.

"I don't know what it means," I admitted. "But I'm pretty sure there's something weird going on."

"Pretty sure?" Rouge blurted out, nearly laughing. "You can't be serious? This has *monsters* written all over it."

"Yeah, but I don't know how it could be. Not for certain." Sure, there were things bubbling in my mind, pieces of pieces, a puzzle laying before me just waiting to be put together, but I wasn't sure what the whole picture would make up. I wanted to sit down, maybe try and lay out everything we knew so far, and then I could try to start connecting the dots.

"Well, I have some thoughts too, though to be honest, I don't know as much as you do," Rouge said to me as we stepped out of the wooded area.

"Well, let's find out where we're going to stay tonight and we'll try and hash it all out and come up with something."

"Stay the night?" Garcia asked as we approached the car. "Why aren't you staying at either of your places?"

I gave Garcia the highlight reel of everything that had happened with Parks, as best I could without telling him that we'd murdered him—well Rouge had—and had in fact done it twice. It's not that I wanted to keep it all a secret from him; it was more going through the whole story would just take too long. Better to keep it low and slow.

"You two could stay with me, if you want," Garcia offered, and I was already shaking my head. He lived in a good size house, but also lived there with his wife and children. I didn't want to go there, just in case Parks did somehow manage to find us. It would be harder to fight him if we had to worry about them too.

"Thanks for the offer," I said to him. "But I think for safety reasons it's better we don't put your family in danger. This Parks guy is a cockbag."

"I wish I had a chance to meet him when we grabbed him for you," Garcia said, and opened the door for Rouge. "Is there anything I can do to help you? We have his photo from the arrest. I can put out an APB for him."

"I don't think that will work," Rouge said with a chuckle, and I shot her a look.

"Why not?" Garcia asked.

I didn't want to let her answer, and say something that might force us to try and explain things clearer than we already had. "He's not human, and he's been changing his form since you guys let him go." It was the best I could come up with.

"Well, that's got to make things pretty hard to hide from him."

"It's why we were planning on moving out to the sticks," Rouge said, and explained our plan a little to him. He thought it sounded like a great idea. "But don't worry, Detective, we'll do our best to help you sort this out before we move into our hobbit hole."

"I appreciate that," he said, and saw us off.

As we drove off, passing the media on the way, Rouge turned on the radio, but I quickly shut it off. She tried to turn it back on, but I stopped her, and she gave me a look.

"Why are you interfering with my music?" she asked sarcastically. "You never interfere with a woman and her tunes."

"You almost said too much back there," I said to her, ignoring the joke.

"About what? Parks?"

"Yeah. I'm not sure we need to tell him every little thing about this. Especially how you killed Parks twice and we melted him in the tub. I'm sure there's a police report out there somewhere about the body we left in the middle of your street."

"True," Rouge nodded, and I could tell she hadn't thought about that. I don't blame her. There's plenty more to think about than that. "By the way, you looked like you were keeping in more from him than just the info on Parks."

"I did, but I didn't. I have some small thoughts rolling around my head, but nothing really substantial. I do think this is one of the most fucked up things I've ever seen. Nothing about it makes sense to me."

"Well, clearly this is the strangest thing I've ever seen, and I sleep with an alien."

"Gross," I laughed. "Who's this alien, and what planet is he from?"

She laughed at that for a moment and then turned to me all serious again.

"So, where are we going to go for the night? I want to snuggle up somewhere nice that doesn't involve an anti-bacterial scrub down, so we can get our Nancy Drew and Hardy Boys on."

I hadn't bothered to make any reservations yet, and had no idea where to stay, so I pulled over and made a quick check on Expedia to find something that would give her a smile. I had to admit, it was for me, too. Sleeping in those scrubby motels, all the funky smells, and the horribly uncomfortable beds; I need some luxury.

Luckily there were some decent motels available, though they were pricier than I had imagined. Well, sometimes you have to spend a little more if you want quality.

"Let's head to our castle now, my love," I said, and we drove west.

"Not even a hint?"

"Not even a whisper."

The motels we had been staying at were about fifty bucks a night. It's expensive for the kind of trash you get. The hotel we would be staying at tonight, the *Windsor Arms at Bay and Bloor*, was way more expensive than that, but the front lobby alone was glorious and well worth it. Instead of being greeted by someone in a dirty robe, who looked as though they didn't want to be bothered with me or my money, the front lobby staff went out of their way to please us. They offered us a seat while the room was made ready, provided tea and a lunch menu in case we were hungry, and gave us some information about a high tea service they offer. This was the fanciest place I'd ever stayed in, and it made me wonder how I'd ever go back to seedy motels again. I was sure the bill at the end of the stay would remind me.

The room was even nicer than the lobby, and Rouge wasted no time flopping onto the bed and stretching out. While she did that, I took a look at the bathroom, complete with a massive jet stream tub, and I knew how I'd be ending my night.

"This is too good," she said, turning on her side to look at me as I stepped out of the bathroom. "Should we order some food, or do you want to do that high tea thing?"

"I'd do the high tea, but I don't have anything nice to wear," I admitted, knowing that aside from an extra pair of clothes I'd normally left at Rouge's house, which were now in my go bag, I had nothing at all. I wasn't sure what she had packed, but I wouldn't have been surprised if she had a full bustle dress in her case.

"It's high tea, darling," she scoffed. "You don't need to really dress up for that, though I have gone full Victorian once or thrice."

I chuckled and we decided to go for the tea, then. I called down to the front desk, was told we could come down in twenty minutes, so we decided to get spruced up before leaving. Once there, we were sat in a cozy, over-the-top room with crown molding, a marble fireplace, and a chandelier Liberace would have been jealous of. We were served tea, tiny sandwiches, scones with clotted crème and jam, as well as some of the smallest, most delicious desserts I'd ever had. I started to talk about how lovely everything was, how it was nice to take a break from the world here, but Rouge wanted to talk shop.

"So, what are you thinking about all that headless stuff?" she asked in a hushed voice, trying to keep the people at the next table from hearing us.

"Well, there's a lot going on there, but I don't think this is the place to start breaking it all down, do you?"

"Why not? Half the city is undoubtedly talking about it. Even the people close to the door were when we walked in. Come on, Dillon. You have to have some ideas. Even I do."

"I'd like to hear yours first," I offered, because I really didn't have much, just traces of an idea.

"I don't want to say yet."

"Why?"

"I don't know. Maybe I don't want to say something dumb, make you think I'm clueless. But if you go first, I might see that we're on the same page and I'll feel better about offering what's rattling around in my head. So, you go first."

I agreed to, and told her the ideas I was sifting through.

"So, what I'm doing is trying to line up what we do know first. We know that all the victims are men, various ages, occupations, races, and education levels."

"And not all are local, but most are."

"Right. We also know that all of them have been found in some state of nakedness, and recently had sex."

"I think that's important," Rouge interjected. "And so is the fact that everyone died in a sort of public place."

"What? They did?" I hadn't really thought about it, but she was right.

"Yeah. They died in alleys, cars, public bathrooms, parks, motels, back of a McDonald's. Not a single victim was found in his own house or apartment."

She was right. I hadn't really thought too much on that part of it. "You think that's an important part of this?" I asked her.

"That maybe these guys all went to a prostitute?" she said reluctantly, and I wondered if that was one of the things she worried telling me, because if it was, she had no reason to. It made perfect sense. I'm sure even Garcia knew it, but I didn't think of that. "It might not be that at all, but it's a possibility. It would kind of make sense, I think."

"You might be right," I told her and nodded, thinking about how it lined one dot up to the next. If all these men had met their killer thinking they were hooking up with a prostitute, it might help us find the murderer. I told her as much, but she shook her head.

"What if it isn't, though? What if there's just a lot of happenstance and conjecture that could lead us the wrong way and make us turn in the wrong direction?"

"It's a lead, something we can pursue until we find the killer, or until the lead is dead. There's no such thing as a bad guess in this work, Rouge. Sometimes you have to look at things, consider even the absurd, and follow it or eliminate it."

"Which brings us to the silicone," Rouge said, and took a sip of her tea. "I've been trying to figure that out, ever since Garcia first mentioned it being on all the victims."

"Me too. There's that, and the foam. Neither of it makes any sense, especially with the finger found at the last scene. There's no doubt that it'll come back as the same silicone found on each of the victims, but what does it even mean?" I had been thinking so much about it, coming up with nothing no matter what I did. I thought it might be some sort of lube, or something the killer might've worn when committing the crime. That was all thrown out the window once the finger was found.

"What if the killer had some sort of prosthetic arm? That would explain the finger." I laughed and Rouge blushed as though embarrassed. "I know. That's dumb, right?"

"Not at all. I actually love the way your mind is working. A prosthetic arm. I'm not sure I would've ever considered that," I wanted to call Garcia right there and tell him what she just told me, but it could wait until after we were done with tea. "Do you think there are any arms that have some sort of hydraulic system in them that could squeeze and crush, maybe—"

"Rip someone's head off?" she finished for me. "I thought that too, but don't these creatures and demons come through in spirit form and then pull inanimate objects to them to form bodies?" I nodded, and worried that nothing was ever going to come together easily. She was making complete sense, and then boom, things fall apart again. Of course it doesn't always work that way. I thought of the demon in Niagara Falls, and the one that had taken over my friend not that long ago.

"Unless wherever the monster came through was some warehouse or shop that houses silicone body parts. Like a movie FX company, or something like that. The whole thing could be made up of discarded prosthetics," Rouge added, and though it might seem like a stretch, it did give me some hope. I let out a breath, but then Rouge shook her head and decided to add a little more to it. "There's still one part that doesn't add up there. The foam on the wound is the part I don't get."

I opened my mouth to say something, but there was nothing to add to that. I hadn't made any headway with what it could be either, but I had smelled it and there was something I knew there, a familiarity to it that was on the tip of my tongue. I felt my jacket pocket; the pen was still there. I took it out, saw what was on it, dry now, and gave it a whiff. That smell was still there; something about it reminded me of the outdoors, and summer, but what?

"What are you doing, Dillon?" she asked, giving me a strange look. I guess pulling out a pen and sniffing it when you're having high tea in a fancy place might look a little weird.

"This is the pen I used to touch the stuff on the last guy's neck," I told her, and held it out towards her. "There's something there, a scent, that I know but I can't place."

"I'm not smelling your pen right now," she said, and looked around the room. "Maybe just tuck that away for now, and when we get upstairs to our room, you can pull it out for me. The pen, I mean," she winked. "Or maybe that too."

I put it away and we finished our tea and food. Once done, we headed back to the room and when I handed her the pen, she made a face and passed it back to me.

"What the hell is that?" she asked, her face scrunched up in what was clearly disgust.

"That's what I want to know," I said, and smelled it again. "There's a thing there, something familiar, but for the life of me, I can't place it."

"It smells like a squashed bug to me," she said, and wiped at her nose. "I don't know what it is you're picking up, but that's all I'm getting from it."

"Squashed bug?" I asked, and sniffed it again.

"Yeah. It smells like when you accidently crush a grasshopper or ladybug."

I could see what she was saying, but it didn't help me with

this. Why would the foam on the neck smell like a squashed bug? I tucked the pen back into my coat, figured I could take this one thing at a time.

"So, is there anything else you'd like to pull out for me?" Rouge asked and sat down on the bed. "Anything at all?"

I did have something in mind.

Thursday

After waking up we ordered a big breakfast, and then I gave Garcia a call. It went straight to voicemail, so I left a message telling him to call me back as soon as he could. While we ate in our room, I turned on the TV and flipped it to the news. Every station we tuned to, it was all the same story. The talk of the town was all about the latest murder, and most stations spared no small detail for their early morning audience. They gave a recap of the previous murders, and capped it off with the gruesomeness of the latest one. They mentioned the names of all the people killed, how their heads had been taken—and still not found—and how there had been signs of sexual activity before each of them passed.

It was amazing how the media divulged that kind of information, especially at such an early hour in the day. Nothing goes with toast and coffee quite like dismemberment and sex. I watched despite my urge to flick the TV off, just to see if the reporters might say something we didn't already know, give me something more to go on than Rouge and I had already discussed.

I really wanted to believe that the points we made might lead to something big. I hoped to talk to Garcia soon, bounce the ideas we had off him and come up with a plan. I wanted to help as much as I could, to firstly find out who or what was doing this, and take it from there. I hadn't forgotten about Parks. The hunter was relentless, and forgetting him would be the end of me. Literally.

Rouge took the convertor from me and switched the TV off.

"There's never anything good on the news, Dillon. Let's not start off the day with a load of that garbage."

"I just wanted to see if there was anything about the case," I told her, and moved to take the converter back, but she shifted it out of reach.

"They're not going to tell you anything that Garcia hasn't, or that you didn't see yourself. It's the news after all. They bottom feed, report on the worst things they can. They lead with any and everything to scare the shit out of you, and then end with some puff piece about a dog that can skateboard, or a cat who knows how to use the toilet."

"Next thing you're going to start calling them fake news," I laughed, and tried for the remote again.

"Ugh, don't lump me into that, Dillon. The only thing I loathe more than news, is politics," she said and stuffed the remote down the front of her top. "Now let's drop this news thing and talk about something better. Where do we have lunch today?"

"We haven't even finished breakfast," I joked, and pointed to the tray of food in front of us. "Are you already thinking of lunch?"

"Well, after the great tea we had, I thought we might have some more fancy meals here, or somewhere close by. We're really close to Yorkville, and that's where all the celebrities hang out."

I shrugged. I wasn't sure I wanted to do something as public as walk around the Village. Between Parks hunting us, and the YouTube video still trending, I didn't really think we should tempt fate, even with us dressing down at the moment.

"Maybe eating here would be better," I suggested, and hoped she wouldn't insist on celebrity sightseeing.

"You're probably right," she said and nodded. "I nearly forgot about the madman hunting us. It's funny how that is. So busy thinking about this case, the man I killed twice just completely slipped my mind."

"It is funny."

"So, then, what's the plan for the day?"

I told her what I hoped to do, which was pretty simple: speak to Garcia, sort some things out, and laze about our very expensive hotel. With the price we were paying for the place, we might as well enjoy the hell out of it. She liked that idea. I could tell by the way her eyes lit up.

First though, we needed to finish our breakfast and wait for the detective.

Garcia didn't get back to us until nearly eleven in the morning. I'd almost all but given up, thinking we were going to end up having lunch before we heard back from him. When he called, he sounded tired and haggard. He told me he'd been forced to have a meeting with the higher- ups, and after that was part of a press conference that was as much fun as an open casket funeral. Apparently the reporters ate him alive, were just completely unrelenting with their questions, calling him and the rest of the force incompetent.

"Sorry about that, Garcia," I said offering as much as I could in the way of condolences.

"Yeah, well, the sooner we solve this case, the better I'll be," he groaned.

"Unless this does turn out to be some sort of monster; then it'll be a little hard to explain it to the media and your bosses."

"Shit. I hadn't thought of that. Thanks for making my shitty day a little bit worse," he said, and I apologized again, this time for myself. "Well, I hope you have something better to say than that."

"I might. When we left you, I started talking some of this out with Rouge, and we have some ideas, pieces of a bigger picture maybe. There's nothing for certain, but they're some ideas. Do you want to meet up so we can go over it?"

"Sure. Anything to get out of the office at this point. Where are you?"

I gave him the address and room number and less than thirty minutes later there was a knock at our door. We asked if he wanted anything to eat, and when he said he did, I ordered room service for all of us, deciding to talk about it all over food. The meal didn't take long, and when it arrived, we began. I gave him everything we had put together. We started off with the whole prostitution thing, and he nodded right away.

"That's the ongoing theory we have, too. The way none of them have been found in homes, a few of them have previous arrests with other hookers, but there's something else I don't like about that. None of them were wearing condoms, which isn't the smartest move when having a business relationship with a sex worker."

"Any sign that someone might have taken the condoms after killing them?" I asked, thinking that might the answer.

"No. None of the victims had any lube or latex remnants on them, but they also didn't have any DNA other than their own. No saliva or, well, you know, secretions," Garcia said, and I could see something cross his face that could have been embarrassment.

"That word sounds grosser than pussy juice," Rouge cut in, making a face.

"But that is strange," I added, and turned to the idea that the reason there was no DNA was that it really wasn't a human with these victims. "Was there any of that foam, or silicone, found on the men's genitals?"

"Ugh, just say *dick,*" Rouge groaned again. "We're all friends here, and I'm not some delicate flower. So if one of you says *vagina,* I'm smacking you with these noodles."

"Fine," I chuckled. "Was anything found on their dicks?"

"No foam, but we did find very small amounts of the silicone," Garcia told us. "And this morning I was told there were trace amounts of blood detected on that finger you found. Blood came back belonging to two of the other victims, so there's that."

That was huge. Finding no DNA on them there, but instead more of that silicone stuff was one thing, but finding the blood belonging to a couple of the other victims on the finger was a big thing. The more I heard, the more I was sure the killer was not human, but something that originated far from this planet. And what Rouge and I had theorized, about the monster being made up of silicone body parts and other things, was starting to make more and more sense. I told him that much, explained our theory, but as I did, something about it bothered me. Like I've said before, there was a time when things used to be so much easier, but these days, nothing was black or white. There was always more to it than there should be, a twist to miss, a part that made no sense.

"What's wrong?" Rouge asked, clearly seeing the wheels turning in my head.

"I don't know. Something just seems a little off about what we've come up with."

"How so?" Garcia asked, and sat back in his chair. "I think you've nailed it. Some monster, using some silicone stuff to make its body up, is going around and killing people. Cut and dry. Now we just have to find the thing."

"Right, but I don't think we're totally right about the makeup of the creature. These men, all the victims, they seemed to be willing parties in what happened. If some monster came along, made up of random body parts, why would these men go off with it, or invite it into their cars and have sex with it?"

"Trust me, Dillon, men in this city—hell, men anywhere—will fuck damn near anything that moves," Rouge said as she frowned. "I think if zombies were a real thing, people would find a way to make it sexual."

"That might be, but neither of you have actually ever seen what these things look like. When they form their bodies, they don't look like people. They resemble whatever they were in their original states. I can't imagine someone looking at a silicone version of Frankenstein's monster and wanting to have sex with it."

"Well, what other choice is there?" Garcia asked, and all I could do was shrug. I had no idea. While I was ninety-nine percent sure the killer wasn't of this world, I couldn't wrap my head around how it might do what it was doing, or why it killed the way it did. I tried to think of some sort of monster out in the universe that stole heads or just had a tendency of ripping them off. I knew a few that did, like the Gortho, but they were demon bounty hunters. They wouldn't do that to humans. Especially not the way these victims were killed. "It's either something made up of weird silicone body parts, or there's some sort of praying mantis monster out there eating the heads off people they have sex with."

"What did you just say?" I said, my heart jumping in my chest at his words.

"A praying mantis monster?"

"Shit! How could I've missed that idea?" I pulled the pen from my pocket, the one I'd used to touch the foam, and smelt it. I remembered what Rouge said about it smelling like squashed bugs, and how I thought of the summer, and we were both right. I offered it to Garcia and asked him what he smelt.

"Ugh! It smells like that shit a grasshopper leaves on you when you catch one," Garcia said, and held the pen away from his face. "I used to go to the lake when I was a kid, catching snakes and grasshoppers. My brother used to say it was their shit, and it smells like it could be. Your pen smells just like that."

"Right. It's what they secrete. All bugs have it, usually mixed with some sort of pheromone. And if that's on each of the victims, then we're dealing with Chornaks," I told them, and as I said it, things were really starting to make sense. "They're a species like this planet's praying mantis, that mate and eat the heads off their lovers. Only, the male version of a Chornak can grow his head back, something humans can't."

"So you think it might be them?"

"It fits. Although, they are a strange-looking creature. On their planet, they stand straight up close to seven feet tall, but normally walk hunched over. They have huge, elongated heads with jagged horns running up and down their skulls. If anyone saw one here, in their natural state, or however they made themselves to look when they came to Earth, I can't imagine someone letting it into their car and going down a dark alley."

"Okay, then what?"

I shrugged. There was no easy answer for this, but we had more than we did on his arrival. I sat there, eating more of the food, and considered it all. In the end, all I could suggest was that we start hitting areas that were populated by prostitutes. Since all the victims had been found in or close to areas where prostitution was common, it seemed like the best place to start.

We could park or drive down streets looking for someone or something out of the ordinary. I didn't think we should ask around too much, even though that was Garcia's suggestion. I was certain that doing this all low key was the way to go.

"But what are we really looking for?" the detective asked, and I could hear the frustration in his voice.

"We know this thing is made up of silicone, at least partially. Between the finger, the stuff on the wound, and also because it was on their dicks, we can assume the majority of them is made up of that. But seeing as a Chornak is very strange-looking, compared to how humans look, they shouldn't be hard to spot."

"What if..." Rouge started and then trailed off, her eyes moving over to the window as she was clearly thinking about something. I had an idea that she might think it was another silly thought, so I offered encouragement, reminding her that nothing was ridiculous. "Well, what if the creature doing this isn't the one having sex with them? What if these people were seeing regular prostitutes and then were attacked by this Chornak?"

"But that doesn't explain why there is no other DNA on the victims," Garcia said and made a good point. "If these victims were with human prostitutes, there would be some evidence on them of either sexual contact, or even using a condom. There was nothing."

"Then maybe the humans are luring the victims somewhere, somehow working with the monster. Is that possible, Dillon?"

I didn't know. It could be possible. It wouldn't be the first time a human and creature or demon had worked together for a common goal. In fact, there were dozens of times throughout my time on Earth where just such a thing happened. Her suggestion was a good one to keep in mind, because even if we patrolled areas known to have a large number of sex workers, there was no guarantee we'd ever see the Chornak itself.

"I think it's something to consider," I nodded finally. "But I think doing some surveillance tonight might give us something to go on."

"How do we do it then? All in the same car, or in multiple ones to cover more ground?" Garcia asked.

"How many different areas in the city are there where prostitution is rampant?" Rouge asked, and I watched as Garcia smiled and shook his head.

"More than you'd think," he began to explain. "Some of them even have terrible names like *Hamburger Hill* and *The Titty Trail*. It's vile the way people try and degrade others who are in the sex trade. I know it's illegal, and as a cop I'm supposed to have zero tolerance, but in this day and age, people having sex for money is the least of our problems. That being said, there are ten major areas where you can drive by and see someone on a corner offering themselves."

"Ten?" Rouge said, sounding shocked.

"Yeah. Ten that I can think of right off hand."

"Then we should totally split up and try to hit as many of them as possible."

I agreed, but I didn't like the idea of none of us being together. There was too much that could go wrong, too many ways for someone to see something, but not be able to do anything about it. Garcia said the same, but he also didn't like the possibility of another body turning up by the end of the night. With the heat he was getting from his bosses, and that the entire police force was taking from the media and the public, he said he was willing to do almost anything.

In the end, we decided to go in two separate cars only. Rouge would go with Garcia in his car, and I would go in the Jeep. We would also hit areas close to one another like Moss Park and Regent Park, or two parts of Parkdale that were still busy. At least with the way we split up, there would be the proper weapons to deal with a Chornak: me with my Tincher, and Rouge with Parks' knife. That was something, at the very least.

We waited until it was dark to head out. I was still apprehensive about splitting up, but couldn't see any other way around it. We decided something to keep things safer would be to stay in contact with each other. We didn't have radios, so the best we could do was use headphones and stay on the phone together during the entire time. I suggested it be Rouge and myself, just in case I wanted to whisper things to her to make her blush as she sat in the car with Garcia. I didn't tell her that, of course.

"You sure this is a good idea?" Garcia asked, as we stood outside the Windsor Arms.

"I don't know," I admitted. "I figure it's our best bet at tracking down the killer, especially if it's a monster like I think it is. There's no way we're going to find it otherwise, unless someone calls about seeing it and we can find where it is hiding during the days." I pulled my phone from my pocket, to see if there was anything new. Since all the madness with YouTube, I kept my phone on *Do Not Disturb,* but there were no new calls. That was the first time in weeks that I'd gone twenty-four hours without a single call. That could be a good sign.

At that we split up. I took the Moss Park area, focusing on Gerrard Street to Queen Street East, and Sherbourne Street to Parliament. It was a big area, full of low-income housing, drug dealers and users, and prostitutes. Two of the victims had been found close to here, so it was my hope that I'd be the one to find them. Rouge and Garcia took another large area, covering Gerrard to Wellesley Street East, and Church Street to Jarvis. That area had one of the victims, so they might have just as much luck as I did.

"You stay safe," I whispered in Rouge's ear as I gave her a hug. "Don't you do anything stupid or dangerous, and I promise I'll do the same."

"If we see it do something, do we wait for you?" she asked, and pulled out the blade she'd taken from Parks.

"Depends on where I am," I told her, knowing that if they saw something and someone's life was at risk, she would have to act. I didn't want anyone else to die, so I told her to do what she felt like she had to in order to keep people safe. "I love you," I whispered and pulled away.

"I know you do. The feeling is mutual, lover." She smiled and winked, and we got in our cars and headed out. The second Garcia's car was out of sight, I called her phone.

"Can't get enough of me, can you?" she said as she answered.

"Guess not," I admitted, and drove south, and then east on Gerrard.

The streets were busy with life that night. Between those heading home or out for the night, and those living outside the constraints of society, there were more people out and about than I expected. I wondered if it was still too early to find people looking for company.

"Well," Rouge said through my headphones. "We just passed a place Garcia said is called *Hooker Harvey's*, and there are already three looking for Johns there. Anything on your end?"

"Not yet," I told her. "But I think I'm going to add George Street to my area. I can already see it's pretty busy there, and I just realized that the *Filmore* is there, and people leaving a strip club might be looking for some quick action."

"Sounds like a plan."

I drove down the street, saw it was as busy as it had looked, especially between Gerrard Street and Dundas Street East, but maybe it was *too* busy. With all the traffic there, mainly that of drug users by the looks of it, men looking for prostitutes might avoid the area.

After about thirty minutes of driving up and down different streets, I decided to actually stop and watch specific area. I couldn't stay too long in any of them, though, as the police might find me suspicious and start asking questions. Even with Garcia around, that kind of attention I wanted to avoid. There were also the dealers and users whose suspicion I didn't want to raise; especially the dealers. I didn't want them to think I was some undercover cop who was staking them out, or a rival who was encroaching on their area. Getting shot was something to avoid. So, to avoid them all, I'd only stay ten to fifteen minutes here or there, and then on to the next spot.

We were four and a half hours in, and there was nothing to see but the strange show of people searching for the drugs they were addicted to. One woman was acting like a pigeon, bobbing her head back and forth as she searched the ground for what I could only assume was crack. A man who couldn't stop twisting and pulling at his beard repeatedly walked left to right, and then left again in front of a building, scratching his ass and sniffing his fingers from time to time. A couple of men began an argument that nearly turned into a fist fight over a lighter that ended up getting destroyed when it fell. Other than that, I was bored enough to go and get food from a place called *Sam's*. I went in for a pop and some chips, but when I smelt the fried chicken, I was sold.

I paid for it and went back to my car, ignoring the man inside the store asking me if I wanted to buy a cellphone for ten bucks. It was a good deal for an iPhone, but I had little doubt it was stolen.

I was sitting in my car shortly after, still in the parking lot and trying to decide if I would eat there or drive over to Shuter Street and eat while I watched out for our monster. It was tempting to dig in right away, but there was a small group of people who had begun to stand in front of Sam's that made me think it wasn't a good idea. Five men, all twitching like people in need of a fix, so I didn't want to open myself up as a target they might aim at.

As I was starting my car and getting ready to leave, someone walked up to the driver's side window, putting their hands on the roof, and scaring the shit out of me.

"Looking for some company?" the woman asked, and began to lean towards me. As her face came into view, thoughts of the delicious chicken melted away.

"You guys need to head to Dundas and Sherbourne. I'm at a store called *Sam's*," I whispered into the headset. "You need to get here *now*."

"You're a handsome one," said the strange woman with a face that looked as if it was made of silicone, and she did something that might've been a smile. It looked like she was wearing a mask, but I realized it wasn't that at all. Our monster hadn't pulled objects to it to make up its body. Somehow, the Chornak had found one of those Real Dolls, a silicone sex doll, and could walk around looking somewhat human, passable from a distance but horrifying up close. She reached a hand towards my chest. My right hand moved towards my Tincher, and she rubbed me with a hand that was missing a finger. "You look familiar to me. Do I know you?"

"I…I don't see how." I said as I heard Rouge telling Garcia where they needed to go and what was happening. "Are you new to the area?" I asked, wanting to keep her talking.

"Very new," she said, and stared at me with her unblinking glass eyes and a mouth that hung permanently open, ever so slightly. "You sure I don't know you?"

"If you're new here, how would you?" I chuckled and slowly began to draw out my blade, doing it as slow as I could to avoid her noticing.

"You're right. I guess I…" she started and stopped. Her head turned to the side slightly, like a dog trying to understand something they're hearing, and then with lightning speed, her *Real Doll* hands flew at me and wrapped around my throat. "Hunter!" she growled, but couldn't look angry. Her face was frozen in her ever-sexual formed face.

"Hurry. She's getting flirty with me," I choked out, and fully drew my Tincher and attacked the monster's left arm. I slit at it, expecting to cut it right off as it was silicone, but then the knife made contact with metal and could go no further. Shit! Who knew these dolls had a metal skeletal frame?

"You're going to die, hunter," the creature screamed and moved further into the Jeep, squeezing my throat harder and harder.

"You know how many times I've heard that?" I said, as lights started to explode in my vision. I wanted to believe I'd come out victorious in all this, but at that moment, as I tried to cough and couldn't even get enough breath in to do that, I was actually worried.

Well, if I was going to go, I figured it would be better to do as much damage as I could.

I raised the blade away from her arm, listened as Rouge called out for me to answer her, asking over and over again if I was okay, and tore at and cut up the sex doll's face. I watched as bits and pieces of silicone flew from her metal-frame, revealing cold steel underneath. The monster screamed as I did it, yelled at me to stop. I tried to laugh to tell her to fuck off, but I could barely breathe by then. All my strength was being used at the moment to dismantle her face.

"We're here, Dillon," I could hear Rouge saying in my ear through the phone. "I can see the Jeep. We're here."

I couldn't say anything back to her. I knew then I'd be fine, that she'd kill this thing before I got a chance to, and then she could save me for the third time. It wasn't the worst habit I could think of.

As I thought that though, the monster moved even further into the Jeep, and when she did, I took the tip of my Tincher and jammed into in the soft, silicone stomach and ripped upwards. The knife moved so easily until it hit what I assumed was a metal rib cage, but I wouldn't stop there. I meant to save myself, to kill this bitch before she could kill me. I pushed my hand into the cold, soft slit my knife had made in her false flesh, aiming the tip up and up, looking for the center, trying to find the place where the essence of the Chornak lived.

She squeezed harder, no doubt sensing what I was doing.

I could hear a car door slam on Rouge's end of the phone. She was close, but I had this. I would stop the monster myself.

"I'm going to send you back to your filthy body," the Chornak grunted, and squeezed.

"Not if I send you back first," I said, and with a final, weak thrust—that was all I could muster—I hit paydirt and her grip loosened.

"No!" she gasped, her hands falling away. "I can't leave. Not yet. Not alone."

"Too fucking bad," I whispered, my throat aching and burning, and gave it one more push. The Real Doll slumped in the doorframe, hanging half in, half out of the Jeep. I pulled my knife from her before pushing the silicone woman out, and leaned back in my seat trying to breathe deeply again.

"Dillon!" Rouge screamed, and ran over to the same place the Real Doll had just been. "Oh my God, are you okay?"

"I think so," I said softly, and tried to smile at her. "I couldn't very well let you save my life again now, could I?"

Friday

It was after one in the morning when we said our farewells to Garcia. There'd been quite a mess after they arrived, after I had dispatched the Chornak trying to kill me. I was exhausted from the short struggle and the lack of oxygen after being strangled by the monster hiding in the silicone sex doll. It took me more than a few minutes to gather myself, and when I did, I stepped out of the Jeep and saw the small crowd that had gathered around us.

"Did you see that shit, man?" one guy yelled and pointed at the fallen doll.

"Yeah, man. 'Course I did. That motherfucker killed that bitch," another said.

"But she was a freaky looking thing," the first said, and tried to move closer to get a look at her. "And the bitch ain't bleeding a drop."

"Get back, everyone," Garcia ordered, and flashed his badge. "You can stay there all you want, and when the police units arrive, you can give them your names and statements of what you all saw. That is, unless any of you have outstanding warrants when they run your names."

I watched as the group of men, who'd been there since I exited Sam's, exchanged looks with one another. It didn't take a genius to see them start thinking about whether or not they had any outstanding warrants, if they'd missed a court date or forgotten to check in with a parole officer. One second they were watching us, and the next they were moving as fast as their feet could take them without running. I guessed they weren't sure having their names run was such a good idea. I didn't blame them. I wanted to get out of there too.

"Now what?" I asked. I could see other people arriving, curious about what might be going on in the store's parking lot. "Are we really waiting for uniformed officers to show up?"

Garcia laughed. "For what? A chopped-up rubber doll? Look at it."

I looked down at the thing lying by the Jeep, and it might've been one of the creepiest things I'd ever seen. I'd done a number on the face. Most of the left side was missing, jagged tears in the silicone revealing a metal skeleton underneath. It appeared to be offering a strange grin in death, when it never should've been alive to begin with. I nudged it with my foot, the entire body moved, and I wondered how anyone ever got off with the thing. Surely the victims who'd been killed by her had seen how unnatural she looked. There was no way you could look at the expressionless face and not know that she wasn't truly alive, that there was something so off with her.

"We should put it in the Jeep and get out of here," Rouge said, and pointed to more people standing around us. "Someone might actually call the cops over this."

"Yeah, but even if they do, all they'll find is someone who killed their sex doll. No actual crime, aside from maybe trespassing or public mischief, could be pegged on me. Right, Garcia?"

"You're right, but I don't want to have to explain why I was here," he said, and cautiously looked around. "Why don't you two get that thing into the Jeep and I'll pretend to do some police work." I nodded and as I went to lift up the now monsterless doll, Garcia did his best police acting job. "Alright you two, enough of this shit. Clean up this mess and stop making a scene, unless you want to go to jail for the night," he said, raising his voice for the benefit of people who were passing by and looking over.

"What is that?" someone called out, as the crowd close to us, having grown to eight people by then, began talking to Garcia and among themselves.

"It's a doll, I think."

"No way. I saw her walking. That ain't no doll. She's alive."

"Look at it. You think that thing was alive? You're crazy, girl."

"I saw her too. Weird ass chick who wears a rubber mask."

"No way. She's one of them expensive blow-up dolls rich dudes like to fuck."

Garcia walked towards them and held his hands up, telling them to back up. "Let's go, everyone. Nothing to see here. Just some people trying to make a viral video."

"Bullshit!" a woman yelled.

"Oh damn, it's that monster cop dude. The one from the distillery."

Great. Just what I needed.

"Oh wow, you're right! It's the Dick Monster. Come on, Betty, this shit is fake. It's just like the other video. These YouTube fucks are always trying to do stupid stunts like this to get likes. I'm out."

And with that, the crowd started to get out of there. Finally, that video was working for me. It was about time. The thing was a thorn in my side, but in this case, it might be the one thing I needed. As soon as we saw most people were no longer that interested in us, Rouge and I lifted the heavy, dead monster that was only a doll now, and put it in the back of the Jeep.

"Jeez," Rouge whispered, and slammed the door as she struggled for breath. "This thing is heavier than Parks was."

I shot my eyes over to Garcia, worried he might have heard what she said, but he was still busy with the last of the crowd. "You need to stop saying that out loud."

"Oh, it's not like he heard us. I was quiet."

"Still, what if he had?"

She shrugged and didn't seem bothered at all by the thought. I was trying to keep it a secret. I didn't want anything bad to happen to her, even if it was short term. I knew in the long run Garcia would end up understanding, but he was also a cop, and there were only so many things he could ignore.

"You two need to get out of here," Garcia said when he was done with all the lookie-loos. "What are you going to do with that thing?"

"No idea," I admitted. "Maybe I can find out where it was made, and then I will be able to find the weak spot it came through. It could either be a place that makes these things, or more likely it's someone who owned this. Can you get a list of the houses of all the victims? Maybe we can track them down and see if any of them once owned one of these silicone sex dolls. We should start with the first victim."

"I'll see what I can do, and I'll also run a check and see if anyone reported one of these things stolen. I'm going to assume they cost a pretty penny."

"No idea, but yeah, I would guess the same."

"Okay, well if you figure anything out let me know, and I guess now we just wait for all this to blow over," he said, and sounded stressed-out.

"You okay?" I asked, figuring he'd be happy to know there'd be no more dead people showing up with their heads missing.

"I'm fine. I mean, I'm happy this is all over. Of course I am. But I still have a stack of unsolved murders that are going to stay that way because there's no way to prove what really happened, nor can I tell anyone without being put on a leave for psychiatric evaluation. I almost would have preferred if this wasn't one of your cases, that it was just some psycho stealing heads for kicks. Still, I can't thank you two enough for helping me with this."

At that, we got in the Jeep and headed back to the Windsor Arms. When we pulled into the underground garage, I got out of the Jeep and looked into the back seat. The lifeless, very real looking body the monster once lived in lay there, arms and legs stuck frozen upwards, making it look like a dead bug. I had no idea what to do with it. We couldn't very well take it up to our room—I'm sure people would notice it if we tried—but we also couldn't leave it lying in the back the way it was. Anyone passing by would see it, and they might even call the cops, not knowing it was a doll.

"We need to cover it up," I told Rouge, and asked her to wait there while I went to the room to borrow a blanket. The hotel was quiet and I didn't have to sneak around, which made it easier.

When I got back to the Jeep, Rouge helped me straighten out the doll's arm and legs, and then pushed the heavy body down so it was jammed in the backseat footrest area. We carefully covered it up with the sheet so nothing peeked out. If anyone passed by and glanced in, they wouldn't be able to tell what was in there. Nosy people were everywhere; best not to give them something to make them even more curious.

Once done, we went back to the room and undressed for bed. I was already exhausted and ready for a long, deep sleep, but as I slid under the blankets, Rouge wanted to talk.

"What a night," she said as I turned off the lamp on my side.

"Indeed it was. Want to talk about it in the morning, though? I'm beat."

"Sure, but don't you think that all went a little too easy?"

"I'd say yes, but it's still a little hard to get it out because I was strangled by a sex doll. You think it was too easy?"

"I kind of do. I know you had a fight with the thing, but what are the chances we'd find it on the first try, the first day? And from what you said, the Chornak found you. What are the chances of that?"

"Well, sometimes dumb luck is just one of the best things about this job. When it's big and strange like this, it's usually just luck that helps solve the case. This was clearly one of those," I said, but then my mind started to turn. She was right It was easier than it should be. There were so many areas of the city the monster could have been, victims had been found all over the city, and yet we'd managed to pick the right area on the first try. And we hadn't picked it because of how many victims had been found in the area, we chose it because it was close to us, and it would allow us to stay close to one another. Things used to be this simple, and yet, they never turned out to be quite *this* simple.

I rubbed my throat, thinking about it and turned on my side to face her. "So, what are you thinking?"

"I don't even know, Dillon, but I think we need to find out where the body for the monster came from. There has to be more to it all than just the thing lying in the back seat of the Jeep."

I wasn't so sure. I mean, yes, over the last few years, everything seemed to have a bigger, more complex picture to it. Ever since the Hellion in Innisfil, simple cases had become a thing of the past, for the most part. Not all of them, of course, were as crazy as the Hellion, but when Garcia first contacted me, I was sure this was going to turn into some long, drawn out mess that would end with me having to take a healing bath, or getting a new body. Yet, when I plunged the knife into the sex doll and dispatched the monster, I was happy it wasn't and was already over. Then, in bed with Rouge, I felt as though she was trying to rain on my parade, and make it more than it had to be. I came, I saw, and I slew the dragon. With that done, we could move on, get out of the city and never look back. I didn't really want to look at it any closer, in case we saw something that would ruin our plans.

I said so much to Rouge, and what I got in return was a weak smile.

"What?" I asked, not ready to just let that look drop. "Are you having second thoughts about leaving the city now?"

Rouge shrugged as best she could as she lay there. "It's not that I don't want to leave, it's just…I don't know. I'm a little worried."

"About what? That there's more to this case than the dead doll?"

"It's not that. I think I'm worried about being in the middle of nowhere, hiding away like that; I'll be bored, but more than that, I'm worried you'll be bored. You were so excited tonight. I could see it in you. Hunting is part of who you are. It's what you've always done. What if you get there, in the woods, surrounded by nothing but nature and me, and you get bored with it all, bored with me?"

"That could never happen," I said, and leaned in to kiss her. "Being alone with you is the best reason to go. To me, that sounds like the perfect life."

"And if you can't take being there anymore?" she asked, pushing the conversation instead of letting it die.

"Well, there's a great, big world out there. If we don't like where we are, we'll find somewhere else to go."

"Promise?"

"It's more than a promise."

When we woke, we packed our things up, and got ready to head out. I was still trying to figure out where we were going to dump the body in the back of the Jeep. Rouge thought we should just drive to some building and throw it in a dumpster, but then I imagined someone going to throw out their kitchen garbage and seeing it there; they'd call the police, assuming it was a real dead body.

"Maybe we should just leave it where it is for now, and when we finally settle down we can bury it," I suggested, because no other way seemed good. Each possibility and idea I had brought me to the idea of some poor soul seeing it, freaking out, and wasting the time of the police with a 911 call.

"You want to bury the doll?" Rouge asked, and there was a sound of humor and sheer disbelief in her voice. I'm not sure that if she had been the one to suggest it to me, I would've acted any different.

"I know it's weird, but I don't want to just be some sort of dick who dumps it somewhere that allows people to find it. It'll freak someone out, maybe even a kid."

"I see your point. So, that's it then? We're leaving the city?"

"Yeah. I think it's for the best we do it now."

"Well then, rambler, let's get rambling,"

We went down to the lobby to drop off the key and check out. It was much better than our last experience, first off with them being right at the desk, and then seeming genuinely happy to see us. We paid up, and were on our way to the garage when Rouge suggested we go for breakfast first. She asked the clerk where a good place to eat was, and she offered a suggestion of a place three blocks away called *Rumble Tums and the Fat Chef*. I chuckled at the name, and we decided to head out. Before we did that, we dropped off our bags, leaving them in the Jeep on top of the body that wasn't really a body but still gave me the same guilt complex as if it were.

The restaurant suggested to us was tucked in between two clothing stores on Bloor Street West that sold hold high end garments. It was small, and cozy, and busier than I was expecting. We had to wait about ten minutes to get a seat, but once we ordered, the food came out fast, and was well worth it. Over the bountiful meal, we talked about nothing more exciting than the names of towns we might want to try moving to, and how many bedrooms we wanted, or if we actually liked the idea of getting a yurt. It would be easier to buy land and get one of those than it would be to find a house. I'd once bought a house many years ago, and there was quite a process to it all.

When we were done, we headed back to the hotel to get our car and get out of Dodge. The day was already turning out to be an amazing one. The sun was out and bright, the breeze cool, and the wonderful food still lingered on my tongue. I took Rouge's hand, and she kissed me on the cheek.

"Hey," a woman said as she passed us, doing a double take. "Aren't you a monster hunter?"

I groaned; the stain of that YouTube video was still on me. I stopped and turned to say no; as I did, I was knocked to the ground, and felt the weight of the woman on me. I had no idea what was going on, but for a brief second I was sure it was the silicone sex doll we'd left in the back of the Jeep, filled up with another monster, or the same one, hungry for revenge. I struggled to see her face, to get her off me, and as I did, I saw a flash of steel in the sunlight and knew there was a knife in her hand.

Somewhere in the distance, I heard Rouge yelling, telling her to get off of me. That's what I wanted too, but she continued to push down on me, growling like a wild animal, and did her best to get the knife in her right hand in between us. I could see her face at that point, knew she wasn't the doll. This was an actual woman. She was maybe forty-five to fifty years old, with greying hair, and hazel eyes. I had no idea why she was attacking me, using all her might to stab me, but then, suddenly, I understood.

"Get the fuck off me, Parks!" I yelled, and tried to headbutt her/him, but to no avail. There was nobody else who would call me a hunter, and then try to turn me into a pin cushion, than Parks.

"Parks?" she said, and stopped struggle for a second. "Who or what is Parks?"

Oh, that came as a surprise.

Though that one was quickly taken over by the shock of feeling the knife she was holding slide into my stomach. I cried out and grabbed her wrists to keep it from going any deeper. My skin around the blade began to burn as the steel was jostled back and forth inside of me.

"What the fuck is your problem?" I said through winced teeth, staring into the face of the mad woman.

"You're my problem," she cackled. "You need to die, monster hunter. You all need to d—"

Her words evaporated on her lips and her eyes rolled into the back of her head. She went limp on top of me, driving the blade down, and I had to move quickly to avoid it going in all the way. She toppled to the side, and standing over me was Rouge, holding a rock she must've taken from a planter close by. She looked terrified.

"Are you okay?" I asked her.

"Are you? Jesus, Dillon, there's a knife in you."

I looked down and saw it. There was at least four inches of blade sticking out of my belly, and it felt like triple that inside. I went to pull it out, but Rouge stopped me.

"You can't do that," she said. "You could make it worse."

"Don't worry, buddy," a man in a nice suit said to me, holding out his cellphone. "I already called 911. Just hold on."

Shit, this guy just made it worse.

I looked around and there were people everywhere. This part of Bloor was busy with the office types. Many of them had cellphones out too, but at least none of them looked like they were taking video. They all seemed to be making calls. I needed to make one, too.

"Rouge," I said, and she got down beside me. "I'm clearly not going to get out of here like this, so I need you to call Garcia right away and tell him to get here, or to at least call whoever shows up."

"Why? Why not just let the cops get her, and then you can go to the hospital?"

"No. I can't go to the hospital. There'd be too many questions.

If they run tests on me, they'll see something is wrong and that will lead to more tests, and a whole mess of problems. Call Garcia first, and when you're done, I need you to call another number on my phone. You'll find his number under *Med*."

"Who is he?"

"Just do it for me, please," I asked, and thought I could already hear sirens in the distance.

I tried to shift my body. The ground under me was hard and unforgiving. I couldn't get comfortable, especially with a knife in me. I instead attempted to distract myself, and looked over at the woman who had done this.

She wasn't moving. There was a bit of blood on her face and I wondered if that was from me, or was caused by the strike to the head Rouge had given her. I couldn't understand why she'd attacked me. I assumed it was Parks, in a new body, and that would've made sense, but she'd looked so confused when I said the name. What did that leave? Was it possible that this was some dead woman taken over by a demon or a monster, just like what happened not too long ago to a priest friend of mine? The only other option was that it was just someone who was not all there in the head, who'd seen the video on YouTube, and thought I was the bad guy.

In this day and age, anything was possible.

"You okay?" Rouge asked me as she put my phone away.

"As good as I can be," I said and winced, as speaking made the blade move.

"Do you know who she is?" Rouge asked and I shook my head, not wanting to expand on it, trying to talk as little as I could. "You don't think that's Parks, do you?" Again I shook my head. I mean, there was no way to know for certain. It could be him and he was just messing with me. The guy was a walking, talking dick. "Well, you know this counts as me saving your life again, right?"

I laughed, but stopped as it hurt too much. "I guess you're right. I owe you another one."

A siren chirped on the street behind us, and I looked past Rouge to see a marked police cruiser pull up. I guess it was too much to hope that Garcia would beat them out. Two uniformed police officers quickly stepped out of the car, and first thing they did was tell the crowd to back away to make a clear path for the ambulance when they showed up.

"Ma'am? Can you step away from him, please? Did you see what happened? Who is this woman?"

Rouge stood up and walked over to the officer with a million questions, while the second one attended to me.

"Are you okay, sir?" she asked, and took hold of my wrist and began to take my pulse.

"Aside from the knife in my stomach, I'm just dandy."

"Well, jokes are a good sign. Can you tell me what happened here?"

I could, but what truth did I want to give her? I didn't want to tell her anything really, but there was so little I even knew. So, I did what I could and gave her the bare essentials of it, the details of the attack, and nothing more.

"Do you know her at all?" she asked me, and I shook my head. "Did she say anything to you?" Not that I was willing to share, so again, the head shake. "And you said that woman there is the one who stopped her, after you were stabbed?" I nodded. "How did she do it?"

"I'm not sure, but I think she took a rock from over there," I said and pointed to the planter.

"Okay, I'm going to need your names," the officer said, and took out a memo book from her bulletproof vest pocket. "Let's start with yours."

This was something I didn't want to say. I knew she wasn't going to let it drop though, so to kill time, I winced and cried out in pain, which ended up causing real pain. She told me to take it easy, to relax, and I nodded and pretended I was going to try, but all I was doing was stalling.

"Sir, what's your name and date of birth?" she asked, waiting on me to offer it, but did she want the name and date of birth I was using, the one on my driver's licence, or did she want my real name, the one my mother gave me more than a hundred years ago? "Sir, can you—" she stopped talking as her cellphone started to go off. "Give me a second, sir. It's my Dispatch calling."

"It's okay," I told her, as though I was trying to reassure her that everything would be fine. In actuality, I was happy the phone rang—saved by the bell—because I was pretty sure I knew who it was.

"Yes, this is Officer Banks." (pause) "Yes, I am with the victim right now." (pause) "Stab wound to the stomach. Knife is still in the wound." (pause) "No. He says he doesn't know her." (pause) "Yes, it was a woman who stabbed him. Older female, grey hair, and—" (pause) "No, but—" (pause) "Yes, sir, but—" (pause) "Okay, sir. If you're sure. I'll secure the scene and get him into the ambulance. They're just pulling in now." (pause) "Not a problem, sir."

The officer stood up and waved to the ambulance that was pulling up behind the police cruiser. She then looked down at me and gave me a stern look. "I don't know who you are, but clearly someone else does. I guess I don't get paid enough to know."

I tried not to smile, but I was so thankful for everything that Garcia must have done to pull that string. I don't have a problem dealing with police—usually, that is—but the last thing I want is some uniform cop trying to earn a detective shield by looking a little too close at my life and my history. It's happened before, and I didn't want it to happen this time. I already had enough to deal with.

"Where's the victim?" I heard a familiar voice say.

"We have two that need transport. The female has a head injury, has been unconscious since we arrived. Male has a knife to the abdomen."

"Okay, there's another bus coming. We'll take the stabbing victim."

"Do you want to check on the woman first?" the female officer asked, and I put on another show of pain to hurry the situation up. "Never mind. Take him."

I was loaded onto a gurney by two EMS workers. One of them I knew, the other was someone I didn't. They moved fast and loaded me into the ambulance gently. As the gurney was secured,

I looked into the face of the medic, Mike, and I gave him a wink. "Thanks for getting here so fast."

"Yeah, well, we better get out of here even faster. We intercepted the call, so there's still two ambulances on the way."

"Who's the new guy?" I asked, motioning towards the man getting into the driver's seat.

"Well, Nikki ended up moving out to Surrey, so I needed a new driver. Hank only came to me a day ago, but he seems like he knows what he's doing. Nobody else wants the job."

Mike the Medic was known by many in the city. He was a legit EMS medic, but he also worked a side business doing jobs for different underworlds, including my own. I'd known him for over twenty years, and he'd helped me out more than a few times. You could always count on him to get there when you needed. In the time I'd known him, he'd gone through quite a few partners, but I would miss Nikki. She was one of the funniest people I'd ever met.

"You have the stuff on you, right?" Mike asked, and at first I had no idea what he was talking about. He must've seen the look on my face because he asked again, and then mentioned the tub, and then I knew what he was talking about. In order to heal myself quickly, even from a near fatal wound, I need to be in a bath with a certain solution. I kept the ingredients with me at all times, in my bag, especially after what happened in Innisfil. Only I didn't have it on me. It was in my go bag, back in the Jeep at the Windsor Arms.

"Look out there now," I told Mike and he listened. "See the redhead? Call her over. Her name is Rouge."

"Ma'am?" Mike called out, and I could hear Rouge out there. "Can you come here, please?"

A second later, Rouge appeared and our eyes locked. I could see the fear and concern in her eyes, but tried my best to smile. I wanted her to know everything was fine, the knife sticking out of my stomach was just an inconvenience, nothing more. She'd seen me worse off, but I was sure it didn't make this any easier.

"Are you okay, Dill?" she asked, and stepped up into the ambulance, coming to my side and taking my hand. "How do you keep getting into all this shit?"

"Lucky, I guess." I tried to laugh, but it hurt too much.

"Dillon, they're asking me all kinds of questions. I'm not sure I know what to say."

"Don't say anything," I told her, and asked Mike to shut the door. "We're going to drop you off at the hotel, and I need you to grab my bag from the Jeep. Remember that bath I took when we first met?" She nodded, and I explained how I needed to have another one, and the stuff I needed was in the bag.

"Are you waiting there for me?" she asked, and Mike shook his head.

"No. We're going to take him to a secure spot and allow him to heal there. I'll give you the address," Mike said, and scribbled down the info for her. "I'm Mike, by the way. Dillon's terrible at introductions, but in this situation, who can blame him?"

"Everyone calls me Rouge," she told him, and they shook hands.

After that, we drove off and left Rouge at the hotel. I gave her the keys and told her to just drive the Jeep to the place I would be. She kissed me on the cheek, and then glanced down at the knife sticking out of me, wiping a tear away as she left us. Once she was gone, we were back on our way.

"Are you two dating?" Mike asked with a sly smile.

"Why?"

"Nothing. I just thought your kind wasn't allowed to date humans. But I guess no rule is worth following for someone who looks like that."

"She's more than just a pretty face," I told him, but didn't say any more than that. Speaking hurt too much, so I wanted to keep things short and sweet. No time to lecture him on how she was smarter, funnier, and more talented than she was beautiful. The fact that humans congratulate others on the looks of their partners was something I would never fully understand.

"I'm sure she is. No offence," Mike said, and began to look at the blade in my belly. "I want to get this out of you and see how deep and bad it is. It's going to hurt, a lot, but at least you'll have an easier time moving without risk of the knife causing more damage."

"You sure?"

"I'm a professional, Dillon. I wouldn't do it if I didn't have to. Now, bite on this and let's get this done."

Mike held a wad of gauze in front of my face and I took it, placed it in my mouth. I bit down on it, and then heard Mike tell me to brace myself. I could feel his hand on the knife the second he put it there, and he counted down before quickly pulling it free.

It felt like fire there. My skin screamed, tingled and throbbed, and I could feel my teeth almost touch, even through the three-inch-thick gauze. I tried not to cry, not to scream, but it wasn't easy. Luckily, it was over quickly, and Mike was putting pressure on the wound.

"Looks like the blade went in nearly five inches," Mike said, and placed the knife down on a tray.

"Is that bad?"

"No way to know for sure. From where it entered and the direction it went it, it may have cut into your intestines, or stomach. There's no way to know for sure without an x-ray, but you won't need one. We just need to get you into that bath, and everything will be fine. For now, I'll patch it up until Rouge gets to the house with the stuff."

While we drove for another forty-five minutes, Mike kept busy tending to me. He checked the wound for any sign of stomach acids, or intestine waste, and when he found none he gave me a quick shot of anesthetic, and stitched me up. He cleaned me, and then put a bandage over it, before he gave me two pills for the pain.

"I'm not sure these will help you much, but for the meantime, you might as well give it a try."

I nodded and took them, and then tried to sit up.

"Hold on there," Mike said and put a hand on my chest, stopping me from getting up. "Let the pills kick in, and then if you're going to sit, you need to put pressure on the wound so the stitches don't pop."

I decided to just stay lying down until we got to the safehouse, which wasn't too long after that. The ambulance came to a stop, and the driver, Hank, called out that we'd arrived. Mike asked him to come around the back and help get me out.

"Where are we?" I asked Mike as we waited for Hank.

"It's a farmhouse that belongs to the Finavera crime family. There's no neighbors anywhere close to here. This place is over seventy acres of property, so we have privacy."

"Uh, Mike," Hank said from outside the ambulance. "I think you need to come and see this."

"Shit! What now?" Mike groaned and opened the door. "Give me a second, Dillon. I'm sure it's nothing."

Mike went out and shut the ambulance door as he did. I couldn't tell what was going on out there, could only hear some muffled words, and a few muffled sounds. I hoped that the people who owned the house, the Finavera crime family, didn't have people out there that might cause a problem. We had enough to deal with as is, without adding mobsters to it all.

A few minutes later, the door opened and instead of Mike coming in, it was Hank.

"Is everything okay?" I asked him as he shut the door. "Where's Mike?"

"He needed to rest for a second, but don't worry, Dillon, I'll keep you company."

I might not have thought anything, may have just figured Mike was dealing with somebody who lived there, if it hadn't been for the blood I noticed on his left hand. Hank had helped me get into the ambulance earlier, and as far as I could remember, there'd been nothing on him. So, where did it come from? I looked from his hand to his face, and when I saw he was smiling in a way that had no humor in it, I started to assume the blood on him was from Mike. Call me paranoid, but it was the first thing my mind went to. I was suddenly sure he'd done something to him, and meant to come after me next. I kept eye contact on him, but with my peripherals, I saw the knife on the tray.

"Just lay down, and when Mike gets back, we'll get you inside the house," he said as though everything was fine, but I knew it wasn't. Call it a gut feeling or a vibe I was getting from him, but there was something not right about the new guy.

Hank stood over me, and opened a cabinet above me. While he was distracted, I quickly reached over and grabbed the knife, moving as fast as I could to hide it at my side. There was something I didn't trust about all this. Hank was rubbing me the wrong way, and I wanted to be prepared for anything.

"What are you looking for?" I asked him, as he searched for something in the cabinet.

"Something Mike said he would need," he said, and didn't even look down at me. I looked at his shirt and pants, and saw there was blood or something like it on his pants, too. What the hell had this guy done?

"So, what did you do before you worked with, Mike?" I asked Hank as he closed the cabinet and looked down at me.

"Before this, I was a hunter, Dillon, but you should know that."

Shit!

Parks!

Something flashed in his hands and came down towards me. I braced myself, raised my hands, knife in my right, and blocked his attack by jamming the blade into his left forearm. He screamed out, thrashed against me, but I fought to push him away. My stomach hurt, pain echoed through me, but I managed to knock him off balance. As soon as he hit the floor, I fought to get to my feet, and made a run towards the door.

I pushed out of the ambulance, out into the day. The bright sun was nearly blinding, but I could hear Hank/Parks getting to his feet. I stepped down, more pain greeting me as my feet hit the ground, and I slammed the door shut. I tried to find something to brace it closed, but there was no point, seeing as there was a second door on the passenger side he could exit from. Instead, I needed to get ready for him to come out and try to attack me.

As I waited, I looked over and saw Mike lying face down on the gravel driveway. There was blood under him, but staring at him for a second showed me he was still breathing. It was a small win, but a win none the less.

The ambulance door opened, and Parks stepped out, a scalpel in each hand. I could see blood running down his arm, pooling at his feet as he stood there, staring at me with a grin on his face.

"You're never going to win this, Dillon," Parks said, but made no move forward. I guessed dying twice was making him be more cautious. "You're only making this worse on yourself."

"You're making it worse. Don't you see that?" I said, trying to plead with him. "This last month alone I stopped a demon who'd attached itself to a woman, and last night stopped a Chornak eating human heads, living inside a sex doll. If you make me go back, whatever is going on here, all this shit happening will get worse and the Collective will only have themselves to blame."

"You are so up your own ass, Dillon. You're not the only hunter on this planet, you know. Others can do what you do without breaking all the rules. Now, drop the knife, and let's end this once and for all."

"Come take it from me," I said, refusing to bow to him. I would gut him first.

"You sure you want to do this?" he asked, still hesitating to end the standoff we were in.

"You sure you don't want to just walk away?"

"I've had enough of this," he said, and he screamed once before he charged at me.

This wasn't good. It was too much like a joust. Both of us had weapons, charging at one another, no easy way to just win. It would need too much luck, so instead of standing my ground, I turned and ran towards the house. I needed to get the upper hand. It was the only way to get out of this unscathed.

I could hear a scream of frustration from Parks as I ran around the side of the house, and headed to the back of it. The place was a massive stone and wood mansion, a cross between an old Georgian home and a log cabin. I could hear footfalls behind me, but clearly Parks wasn't as used to his new body as I was to mine. Even with the stitches feeling as though they were about to rip, I was still able to outrun him. Guess those pills Mike gave me were doing their job.

I managed to get to the back door of the house, glad that it was unlocked, and I went inside, shutting and locking it as I did. I ran through the kitchen, grabbed a second knife I saw sitting on a cutting board. It was big, and looked very sharp. As I stepped through the hall, toward the living room, I heard Parks yelling my name, and then there was the sound of smashing glass.

I needed to come up with a plan, and fast, but nothing was really coming.

That was when I passed a door I figured led to the basement, and opened it. The dark from below called to me, and I knew it was my best play. I smiled to myself, slammed the door, and then waited for my moment.

It didn't take long before Parks stood where I had been, in front of the basement door. He must've heard me slam it, because he opened and cursed the dark. I watched as he was about to step down, and then I came out from my hiding spot.

Instead of going down into the basement, I'd been hiding in a closet across from it, hoping he'd check the cellar first. It's what I would've done if I were chasing someone. It was lucky for me he did, being as predictable as I would be. When he stepped past the doorframe, no doubt ready to slowly descend into the shadows to find me, I quietly stepped out of the closet. I was behind him, and even though I wanted to bury the knives in him and just kill him, I had a better idea. I shoved him with everything I had and he cried out in surprise as he stepped out into the air and plummeted into the dark below. From the top of the stairs I watched him soar, and then go crashing down, splintering cracks filled the air. I had no idea if that was the wooden stairs, or his bones, but I hoped it was the former. I didn't want to kill him, but I was worried I'd go down there and find his neck broken. That's all I needed: another failed plan.

When I heard him crying and asking for help, I breathed a sigh of relief and then turned on the light. It was pretty bad. Parks lay at the bottom, his arms and legs twisted in ways they shouldn't be, blood coming from his mouth and nose, as well as from where I'd stabbed him earlier. He looked up at me, crying, and then turned his head where the fallen scalpel lay. At least I knew his neck wasn't broken.

Slowly, I walked down the stairs. I knew he wasn't faking. There was no possible way he could make his limbs turn in so many different directions. He looked back at me when I was halfway down and pleaded for help, asked me to kill him.

"No," I said, and continued towards him. "I have something else in mind."

When I was done, I headed back outside and checked on Mike. He was still unconscious, but his breathing was steady. When I knelt down beside him, the pain in my side flared up, and I looked down and saw fresh blood had bloomed where the wound was. I lifted my shirt, saw three of the stitches had ripped, but it didn't matter because Rouge would be there soon and everything would be fine.

Mike began to moan a few seconds later, and when he finally came to, he asked where Hank was. I did my best to explain the whole story to him, who Hank really was, and then Mike told me what happened to him. Apparently when Parks had called him out, he pointed towards the house, saying there was someone there, and then sucker punched him, or hit him with something else. I saw a wrench close by and assumed that was what he had used.

"Anything broken?" I asked Mike.

"Doesn't feel like it. Too bad those baths you take won't work on me."

It was a shame, but they wouldn't. I helped Mike up and we headed over to the Jeep to get him cleaned up, and he took some of those pills he'd given me. I told him they worked very well, that I barely felt the cut, or the popped stitches. I lifted my shirt and showed him.

"Well, that didn't take long," he said, and drank some water. "I hope you fucked that asshole up for me."

"Oh, I did something," I said with a smile and said no more because I heard a car approaching. I turned and saw it was Rouge in the Jeep. "Well, here she comes."

When she stepped out of the car, she could clearly tell something was wrong, looking from Mike and then to me. She asked what happened and at first I said everything was fine.

"How is everything fine? Look at you two. And where is the other guy? The one who was driving?"

"Well, that was the problem," I said, and led her and Mike into the house. I took them both into the basement, past the place where Parks had landed, and then over to the far side of the room where I'd left the hunter.

"What the fuck is this?" Rouge said as her eyes found the man in the paramedic uniform, sitting in a La-Z-Boy chair, moaning and struggling. Beside her, Mike began to laugh. "You think this is funny? Why did you do this, Dillon?"

"Because this guy sucker punched Mike with a wrench and tried to kill me. I pushed him down the stairs and then Krazy Glued his mouth shut and his body to the chair. It's because this piece of shit isn't Hank, it's Parks."

"Parks?" Rouge all but yelled. "You've got to be fucking kidding. How did he find you?"

"Well, before I glued his mouth shut, I asked him. Apparently he has a list of people I've associated with over the years, and decided to start getting close to them. As luck would have it, the first one he saw was Mike the Medic."

"Do you think he's the one who sent the woman to stab you?" she asked, walking close to Parks.

"I hadn't thought of it, but you might be right. I don't know what he would've said to her to get her to do it, but I guess it makes sense." Anything could make sense at this point, especially when dealing with monsters, demons, hunters, and living sex dolls with praying mantis monsters hiding in them.

"So, what do you plan on doing with him?" Rouge asked me, and Mike picked up a piece of pipe that was sitting on the basement floor.

"Oh, I know what to do with this asshole," Mike said, and tried to move forward after Parks with the weapon. I held him back.

"Not yet," I told him, and then turned towards Rouge. "Let's go upstairs. I don't want to talk about this in front of him."

The three of us went back upstairs. Part way up, I had to stop and lean against the wall and catch my breath. I was so tired, and knew it was from the hole in my gut. I lifted up my shirt and looked down at it. I was leaking quite a bit, like an old car with a shot fuel line.

"You okay?" Rouge asked, and I nodded. I wasn't, but once we were done talking about all of this, I'd take care of myself.

Once we were upstairs, I went and sat on the couch in the living room. It was a nice one, too: leather, and soft as silk. The whole place was like the couch. Everything was high-end and there I was, bleeding all over the place, leaving a mess. Rouge noticed the place too and asked who owned the house. Mike told her and she shook her head.

"You sure we'll be okay here?" she asked, and Mike nodded.

"This place is a safehouse. If one of Finavera's crew gets hurt, they are brought here, and I help them out. Not my favorite thing to do, but it pays the bills."

I could tell Rouge didn't like it, but she said nothing else on the matter. Instead, she asked me what I planned to do with Parks. So, I paid it out for her. The idea was to just leave Parks here, glued to the chair, maybe even get some duct tape to ensure he stayed put.

"Why?" she asked. "Why don't we just kill him now?"

"What's the point? He knows about this place. He'll just go into another body, and come after us."

"Then kill him for real. Don't you have anything in your bag that will do it?"

I shook my head. "I don't know, but even if I do, all that will do is put me in more hot water and the Collective will send even more hunters after me. Better to leave him here while I get healed, and then we can split."

"Shit," Mike said, and gave me a look like what I just said was messed up. "Do you mean you're going to leave him here to starve to death, because that's what'll happen, right? His body is still human and needs food."

"Yeah, he'll die that way. Not the nicest way to go, but it'll buy me the time I need and then he won't have any idea where we are or where we're going." It was the only plan I could come up with, and made the most sense. Rouge agreed, so from there, we made preparations to get the bath ready and to get me better.

Mike left us, taking my bag and setting up the bath. When he left, Rouge sat down beside me on the couch and put her head on my shoulder.

"I really hope things settle down when we leave here. I love you, but jeez Louise, your life is the craziest thing I've ever seen."

"Things will go back to normal, Rouge. I promise."

How I would keep that promise was a mystery to me.

Sunday

It took longer than I expected to heal. I woke up close to five in the morning on Sunday. The sky was still dark, and the house was silent. I rinsed my body and dried myself off, and quietly walked down to the kitchen. There wasn't much in the fridge, but I found enough to make a cold plate, with a pop on the side. I sat down with the food, so hungry after over twenty-four hours submerged in a healing bath, but I had a thought and took my food down to the basement.

Parks was still alive.

When I got down there, he was secured to the chair with the glue, and with a whole lot of duct tape Rouge must've wrapped around him. I couldn't help but grin seeing him like that, even though I knew in a few days he would be dead. It wasn't as though he'd really die, after all, but he would suffer. And after everything he'd done to us, I couldn't think of someone who deserved it more.

I pulled up two wooden chairs near him; one for my food, one for my ass. As I sat down, the noise must've woken Parks up because his eyes were open and he was mumbling something through his sealed lips.

"I have no idea what you're trying to say, Parks, but it really doesn't matter. You're nothing more than a broken record. All you can say is I must be sent off this planet, I need to stop dating Rouge, I should've followed the rules, but look at you. You're so focused on getting me you got yourself stuck like this. Didn't anybody ever teach you how to do this job properly? You can't follow every rule or you end up dead, crazy, or getting devoured by some ancient demon. I don't break the rules for my own enjoyment, or because I'm just an asshole. Certain rules need to be bent in order to actually stay sane here."

Parks muffled something and even though I couldn't tell what it was, I was sure there were a lot of curse words in there.

"If only you'd been willing to listen to me, to bend those rules you think it's your duty to uphold. If you did, maybe you wouldn't be tied to a chair, waiting for this body to starve to death or to die of thirst. I would've loved to help deal with some of this shit lately, but you're too dumb to know that. So, you win. I'm done with this life. You wanted to stop me, you did it, but just not the way you think. I'm going to leave you here, tied to this chair, and by the time you're dead I'll be well on my way to South America," I said, lying to him, hoping to plant that seed in his head, to make him go on a wild goose chase. "Now, when you come back, you can either take over my spot here, or you can try and find me. But if you do come after me, I will make sure you're never able to get back up again."

Parks mumbled something else, and I nodded while I ate some of my food and took a big sip of the pop. He went silent as I did, and when I turned to look at him, I could see his eyes on my food.

"You must think this is cruel, don't you?"

He nodded and mumbled something else.

"I would give you some, but what's the use? It will only prolong the inevitable. Still, I do feel a little bad for you," I admitted, though if we were talking about percentages of how bad I felt, it would be about 0.00001 percent, and no more. He had tried to kill me, tried to hurt Rouge, and had hurt Mike the Medic. Why did I care if he was suffering? I must be losing my touch. "I will tell you this, and I want you to really listen. Are you?"

Parks' eyes narrowed, but he nodded. He was listening and I was about to lay it all out for him. I'd thought about this long and hard, and I knew that I wouldn't say this to him unless I meant it. I didn't want to threaten him with something I had no plans on seeing through, so I was sure within myself that if things continued down this road, I would do as I promised, regardless of the consequences.

"Upstairs, in my bag, I have quite a few tools. Most of them would do nothing more to you than cause a little pain. But I do have something else. Something I bought from Godfrey a long while ago, but I have never had to use it. I wasn't sure I actually had it with me, but before I came down, I checked and, as fate would have it, it was tucked in there." I watched him closely in the low light as I said. "So, Parks, have you ever heard of a Luzilapsa?"

His eyes shot open, wide, and the fear in them was easy enough to read. I shouldn't be surprised he knew what a Luzilapsa was. After all, shouldn't everyone know the name of one weapon that could truly kill them? A Luzilapsa looks like a small, brass mallet, but is made from metal found on a volcanic planet called Shreez. I had gotten it from Godfrey a few years back, when I thought I would need it to dispatch a demon said to be haunting a graveyard in St. Catharine's. As it turned out, it was not to be a demon, but a man who used a whole lot of meth and thought he was a ghoul. I was glad I had never returned it to Godfrey.

"I can tell you know what that is, and I want you to know that if I ever see you again, I won't hesitate in caving your skull in with it. The fact that I haven't done it yet, that you're only tied up to that chair and will eventually be breathing in a new body, should tell you that I'm not the villain here. By all rights, I should kill you, but there are certain lines I'd prefer not to cross. Do you understand what I'm trying to say to you?"

He nodded, and I hoped he really understood, because even though I really did have the Luzilapsa, I really didn't want to use it on Parks. Killing him for real, not just destroying the body he was in, wasn't something I'd do without considering a whole heap of other options first. Breaking rules was something I was good at; breaking laws like killing another hunter would be my downfall.

"I hope you know, I don't say this lightly, Parks. I don't just threaten you and hope you never force my hand," I told him, doing my best to sound stern and convincing. "I never want to see you again, do you understand me? Do whatever you have to: leave Earth, stay here, but consider our time together at an end. When you wake up in your new body, go out and have a nice meal, and then make your choice. But if you want to live a long, healthy life, do not come looking for me."

When Rouge came downstairs, I'd already made her some breakfast; eggs, toast, and tea. I told her today was the day we would leave, head out to find a new home and start a new life, and she seemed so happy. I was too. After my talk with Parks, I hoped I had actually struck a nerve in him and that we would be done with all this bullshit. There was nothing I wanted more than to sit back, relax, and just do something as simple as watch the sun set.

While we ate, Mike came down and made a coffee and toast and headed out into the living room. He was groggy and sounded grumpy as he left. Rouge was telling me all about a channel she was watching on YouTube that specialized in alternative living—tiny houses, yurts, and buses converted to homes—when I heard a groan from the other room.

"Jesus!" he all but yelled. "Again!"

"What is it?" I asked, feeling a bit concerned by the tone of his voice.

"Oh, nothing to do with you, Dillon. It's just the city. The whole place has gone nuts."

"What now?" Rouge called out, and sipped her tea.

"Two guys were found with their heads missing. One in downtown Toronto, the other in Etobicoke."

And that is how someone ruins your quiet time.

Garcia picked up on the fourth ring and sounded about as crappy as I felt.

"I'm guessing you already heard about this shit?" he grumbled into the phone. "I thought we had the killer."

"So did I," I admitted, knowing the body the Chornak had inhabited was still in the back seat of the Jeep.

"So you think we just got the wrong monster?"

"No. I don't. I'm worried that it wasn't the only one out there," I told him. When I heard the news, it was the first thing I had considered. I wanted to try and say we had simply gotten the wrong creature, but what are the chances that everything else would fit, and we'd just get some other monster? When you considered that some of the murders had happened in different parts of the city, it made sense that there were more than one. The fact that the same had happened last night made me think it wasn't just a second monster out there, either. What was going on? I told Garcia what I thought and he let out a long, unhappy sigh.

"So what do we do now?" he asked, and his guess was as good as mine.

"I think the first thing we should do is meet up, and then we can take it from there," I told him, and we agreed on a time and place.

"You knew about this?" Mike asked when I got off the phone with Garcia.

I told him, and then offered a brief rundown of what had occurred.

"So we're heading back to the city?" Rouge said, and I could tell she was frustrated. How many times could we make plans to leave and then throw them aside? As it turned out, many.

"I think we have to," I told her. I cleaned up the dishes. At the sink, I stood there, looking out the window and imagined not helping anymore. I could put my phone down the garbage compactor, destroy it, and disappear. Wouldn't that be so much easier than trying to find more of these sex doll monsters?

"You're thinking about not going, aren't you?" Rouge said as she came up behind me and put her arms around my waist.

"Is it that obvious?"

"Only because I know you so well."

"I'm as easy to read as a kids' book, I guess."

"More like a colouring book," she said, and laughed. "But

seriously, you know you can't just turn your back on this one. You've seen what these things are doing, and they aren't going to stop. The police aren't able to handle monsters like this. Only you can—with my help, as always."

"Of course. Maybe you can save me one more time."

It was just after one in the afternoon when we met with Garcia at a coffee shop in the Junction area. Mike had already gone back to his life, and Parks was left to die in the basement of the house. We didn't bother to say anything to him when we packed up to leave. What would we say? "Have a peaceful death"? There was no point. We just slipped out of there, the sex doll still covered up in the back of the Jeep, and headed back to Toronto.

"You guys want anything?" Garcia asked as Rouge and I sat down at his table. I said yes, and he called the waiter over. We ordered drinks, and then Garcia started in on the business at hand. "So, we have two dead, same as before. Their pants down, heads gone, no fingerprints, but silicone and foam stuff were found on each body. Just more of the same, right? Or am I missing something here with all of this?"

"No, it sounds like there is another one out there. Maybe two," I admitted, and he didn't take the suggestion well. We had a lucky break catching the first one, but in between finding that doll monster and the murders last night, there hadn't been anything. With so many in such a short period of time, was it possible the creatures were being cautious, or could it be something else?

"So, you think there might be more than one out there still? How many are we talking about?"

I shrugged. There was no way to know for sure. All I did know was this case wasn't over, and I wasn't even sure where to start. Of course, Garcia's next question was "What do we do now?", but I didn't have a clear answer yet. We could go back and do what we had done to catch the first monster, but there was no sure way to know we were in the right area. That first night was the dumbest of luck, nothing more than that.

I asked Garcia if the bodies were found in busy prostitution areas, and he shook his head. One had been, but the other hadn't. The one found in downtown Toronto, in the Moss Park area, was typical with what we'd seen, but the one in Etobicoke had been found on a bike path near the Etobicoke Creek, and it wasn't known for hookers at all.

"Maybe the victim drove them there?" Rouge suggested, but Garcia shook his head.

"Vic didn't have a car, or even a driver's licence. The guy was twenty-one years old, and he was some struggling artist who was still in school. He wasn't very popular among his peers, was a loner. His parents said he had little to no sign of being interested in women, or men for that matter. Not a girlfriend or boyfriend in his life, ever."

"But his pants were still down? Sign of sexual activity?" I asked, and Garcia nodded. "I don't even know what to say about that one, then."

"Neither do I. None of this shit makes any sense to me," Garcia said, and rammed an entire glazed donut into his mouth as though he hadn't eaten in days. "You want to hit the streets again tonight like we did before?" He said added, mumbling through the barely chewed food.

I nodded, and Rouge leaned in. "What about trying to figure out where these dolls came from? I mean, if there were three or more of these things around, isn't there a possibility they all came from the same place?"

She was right. We had talked about that before, but once we had the monster caught and killed, I just figured to let the whole thing drop. Finding where it came from might lead us to the others, give us an idea of where to find them.

"Okay," Garcia said, and pulled out a note pad and began to write some information down. "I can start doing a search into things. Missing dolls, or some warehouse or store that's reported a theft. I would've done that earlier, but I just assumed since we got the one, looking into it any more didn't matter."

"I didn't think it did either," I admitted, and tried to think of anything we might be missing.

"Do you know if these things are even made here, or are they shipped to Canada?" Garcia asked, still writing.

"I don't know, why?"

"Well, if they are shipped here, and the monsters are already inside them, I may have to look at shipping cargo manifests, and any other sources that may have reported things like those dolls missing."

Great; now we had even more headaches for me to think about.

"You do what you can on your end, and we'll check the internet and see if and where there are any local places to buy sex dolls like that. I'm sure it'll be fun," I said, and began to think about the rabbit hole of sex websites we were about to partake in. It might actually be fun, or it could be some of the freakiest shit I'd ever seen. Either way, it would need to be done. I told Garcia to try and run a search as fast as he could, and call me later with anything he found. He asked what I would do overnight, if I was planning on another stakeout. "I think I might, but I guess we'll see what we manage to find."

With that, we left the coffee shop and drove back to my apartment. With Parks out of commission for the next little while, at least we could go to our respective places and get clothes, have a proper shower, and I could load up on anything I could manage to carry. When we walked in the door, Rouge scooped up all the mail that I hadn't bothered with since the whole Niagara Fall case. She skimmed through it all as I went into my room and found a change of clothes. I'd had to take a new shirt and pants from the house where I was healing, and they just weren't my style. At least my coat hadn't been ruined. I loved this coat.

"Anything good in there? Maybe a cheque for a million dollars or so?" I called out, and put on an old *Motorhead* shirt.

"Nothing really. It's bills mainly, and a letter from your building management. Are you behind on your rent?"

I smiled. "No, but you can open it if you want."

I had forgotten the email I'd sent them. Not that it really mattered anymore, especially with the plans we had made. When I had originally sent it out, I wanted to do it as a surprise for her, and now she'd be surprised. I was sure of it. When I heard her make a little happy sound, I knew she got the gist of it.

"When did you do this?" she asked as she stood in the doorway of my bedroom.

"Before all this had happened. I sent it when you first suggested me moving in, before you killed Parks for the first time," I told her as she read the letter over again. I didn't need to see it to know that it was about me ending my lease agreement. Before things had gone nuts, we talked about moving in together. Since meeting her, things had moved fast, but they didn't really head into the move-in-with-one-another idea right away. When she had suggested it, though, it seemed like the natural thing to do. What was the point of us living in separate places when we were spending every day together?

It was all moot now. We weren't trying to figure out if I should move in. The overall plan was to run and buy a new place together. Still, from the smile on her face, I could tell it was the thought that counted.

"You're a very sweet man, you know that?"

"I try."

She put the letter down on the dresser and walked towards me, unbuttoning her shirt as she came. "I know we have some work to do, but maybe we have a couple of minutes to play. You are all better now, right?"

I lifted my shirt to show her the wound was all gone, and then continued to pull it off.

"You can do whatever you want," I told her as her fingers found my skin. "Just don't eat my head when you're done."

We lay in bed afterwards. I was slightly out of breath, and felt out of shape, but it had been a very active thirty minutes. Rouge laid her head on my chest, and I could feel she was breathing just as heavy as I was. At least it made me feel a little better, like less of an old man.

"What do you think we'll do in the country?" she asked, and stroked my chest.

"What do you mean, *what'll we do?*"

"Are we going to grow our own food, maybe start making

and selling crafts in town? I could open up a shop wherever we go. I love to sew, so maybe I could do that."

"What's making you think about this right now?" I asked.

"I don't know. When we were at that gangster's house, I sat out on the porch and walked the grounds while you were healing. It was nice and quiet, but after a while I could see it getting boring. There's a part of me that is afraid of all that peace and serenity. And I doubt you've ever lived a boring life yourself. I don't know if that's a silly thing to say, but it's how I felt."

"Is this back to what you were talking about the other day? Are you worrying about the quiet, or that I'm going to miss being a hunter?"

"No. Not just you. I'm thinking about me. I've always been a city girl, but I used to want to move to the country. There was a time I used to dream of the solitude it would bring, the quiet helping to silence my own thoughts, being able to meditate. But I've never lived a life like that. Everything I know is chaos, and loud, crowded places. What if I was trying to say you'd be bored with being out in the country, when it was really me I was worried about?"

"So you don't want to go?" I asked, surprised, as this seemed to have come out of nowhere.

"Well, you did say you warned off Parks and told him you'd kill him if he came after us, right?" I nodded. "If he listened at all, then why should we even run at all? There's no way he's going to come after you when he knows you have something that could kill him."

I wasn't so sure. Parks had already proven himself to be quite tenacious and thick-skulled. The threat I had made was true, and he did look scared, but how long would that fear last? Would he still come after me, only becoming more cautious and sneakier about it in order to get close without me seeing him? The other issue was if Parks did leave me alone, took the threat as serious as it was meant, how long before the Collective sent someone else to do the job, another hunter I would never see coming? Staying in the city, in the place I'd spent so many years, was a bad choice. We needed to lose ourselves and just disappear. I told her all this, and she was quiet for a long time.

"What now? I guess we should start trying to figure out where these head-eaters are," she said, answering her own question.

"Look, I know you're not liking this," I said, reading how upset she was. "But it's all I can think to do right now. Maybe somewhere down the road, things will go back to normal and we can come back. For now, let's just get out of here; go somewhere quiet where the only thing we need to worry about is if we want plumbing or a composting toilet."

At least that made her laugh.

We got out of bed and headed to the living room. I took up the duty of making some food while Rouge went and grabbed my laptop and started to do some research. I hadn't been gone that long, but long enough that the cream for coffee or tea had gone bad. We'd have to settle for water or pop to go with the toast and eggs I made. While I waited for the toast to finish getting the perfect amount of darkness, Rouge called to me and asked if I knew what brand of doll we had stuffed in my car.

"What do you mean, *brand?*" I asked, as though it was the silliest question I'd ever heard.

"Well, there are five or six major companies that make them."

"That many?"

"I'm sure there are a ton more. Even back when blow up dolls were all people had, there were so many companies making them. Did you see any sort of marking on it?"

"I didn't, but I wouldn't think there would be. Wouldn't that take someone out of the moment, to see the name of some company tattooed or branded onto the skin of their lifeless lover?"

"Well, maybe, but if there's no way to find out the company, how are we supposed to figure where they might've come from?"

"I can go down and see, but just try and find some places around the city that you could buy sex dolls of that quality locally. First, toast and eggs."

We ate in silence, and then I headed down to the Jeep to see. Before I did that though, I walked over to the corner store and grabbed some cream. The pop was fine, but I really needed a nice cup of coffee or tea. While I stood in line, waiting for a man in front of me to buy seventy-five dollars in lotto tickets and cigarettes, I looked to the right and saw the front page of the *Toronto Sun*, the city's closest thing to a tabloid newspaper.

"HEADS ARE GOING TO ROLL. Detectives fail to stop killer, and now have their own heads on the chopping block"

Under the flashy headline was a photo of three detectives, one of them being Garcia. I felt bad for him. I knew he was getting a ton of pressure to solve things, but what made it worse was the fact that even if we stopped the killings, there would be no real conclusion to it all. There would be no suspect like Bernardo, Pickton or McArthur to splash all over the covers of newspapers, a face the media could make infamous. I had one of the killers in my car, but there was no way to show her off to the world and say "This is the doll that has been killing people; you're all safe now." When this was over, and the killings stopped, the media would eventually move on to the next hot topic, but there was no doubt that the higher-ups at police headquarters would still serve one of their own up as a sacrifice. A case this big didn't just disappear.

After paying for the cream, I headed back to my building to try and figure out if there was a marking on the sliced-up sex doll I had hidden away. I walked down the ramp of the garage, and went in. I was careful to make sure there was nobody else around as I struggled to move, lift, and undress the doll and see if there was something to tell me where it had come from. The sooner I could, the sooner we could try and wrap up the case and get out of the city.

I pulled out my cellphone flashlight and moved it over the silicone surface. It was creepy how real the thing looked and, in a way, it made me feel as though I was somehow violating her, even though it wasn't a *her* at all; it was an *it*. Looking at the realistic skin, hair, eye, and details on the hands, though, made it so hard to get past the reality of her/it not being real.

I shook my head.

There was nothing to feel bad about, no need to be embarrassed. I wasn't violating a person, living or dead. It was no different than looking at a model toy or action figure, only this was one people had had sex with, and had also eaten the heads off of those same people. So, there was that.

"Bingo!" I exclaimed when I found something on the right foot of the doll. I moved it closer to my face to get a better look, and when I did, I noticed something moving to the left of my car. I spun my head fast, my heart racing, sure that I was about to be attacked. Instead, I saw a woman and her child walking past. The woman looked horrified and was covering her kid's eyes.

"You should be ashamed of yourself, you pig!" she barked, shaking her head at me and pulling the child away It probably looked terrible from out there. It didn't matter though. I had what I needed.

I quickly tucked the dead doll back between the seat, covered it up and headed back to the apartment with the cream and information. I put the kettle on once I got inside and told Rouge the good news.

"*Ethereal Dolls*," I told her. "There was a name stamped into the foot. Guess you were right."

"Okay, give me a second and I'll check it out."

She went back to typing, and I went to making some hot drinks. When I came back to sit with her, she was shaking her head.

"I can't find anything on them that could help us. They were one of the original companies that made these dolls, but they went bankrupt six years ago. I guess we could try and find out what happened to their old stock, but I'm not even sure I can do that," she said, and went back to typing. "I mean, the company isn't Canadian, so it might be harder to find public records on them, but maybe we can give the information to Garcia."

I wasn't sure I knew what all that was about. The legalities of bankruptcy and the likes was never something I had to worry about. Giving that info to Garcia may be the key, but I still thought it might be good to patrol the city tonight and see if we could find anything. Knowing what we were looking for made it easier than it was the first night. We might even be able to ask around and see if any of the locals had seen any strange, rubber-looking women.

I sent a text to Garcia, and then gave Rouge my plan. We decided to take a nap until it got dark. As we headed to the bedroom, Garcia called and said he would look into it, but he wouldn't be able to join us. He had something to attend at his son's school, and couldn't miss it. He said it was bad enough being in the doghouse with his bosses, never mind with his wife.

"Garcia is going to look into the company records for us. Said it may take a day or two," I told her as we got into bed.

"Is he coming with us tonight?" she asked, and I shook my head. "So it's just *Team Dagger* out on patrol tonight?" she said and I laughed.

"Where do you come up with this stuff?"

"I'm a genius," she said. "But this genius needs some beauty rest."

Monday

We left my apartment at a quarter after midnight. It took us a while to decide where we were going to start. We'd made a list of where all eleven victims had been found and tried to come up with an idea of the best place to start. Downtown still seemed like the best bet as there were multiple spots to hit. We stopped to get some stakeout food though, snacks and drinks because it could be a long night and we didn't want to have to keep stopping off at different places along the way.

Rouge had made a suggestion that she dress a little more provocatively, to find her best "slutty" outfit as she called it, and hang out on the street and pretend she was a prostitute. I didn't like the idea one bit, and shot it down. It was unsafe for so many reasons. If she got into something and I was driving around, too far away, I might not get there in time to back her up. It might not even be a monster who'd come after her. It could be another hooker who thought Rouge was encroaching on her turf, or some crazy person who was looking to carve up prostitutes. After what happened to me in my own Jeep, the evidence of it still on my bruised neck and tucked in the back seat, I didn't want either of us in that situation. We were better off sticking together.

Before we left, though, I went through all my tools and weapons and made sure I had the three things I needed more than anything else: my gloves, which should work on helping to paralyze a Chornak, my Tincher in case it was all I could get at, and a Thurkk, a curved, bronze spike with the bone of a dragon in the center to act as a handle. The Tincher was attached to my belt, and the Thurkk was tucked into the console between us. Rouge asked about it, and I explained that something in the design, the type of bronze used, and the magic whispered into by the Valcareenian who made it would not just stop a Chornak, but would kill its very essence.

"That works for me," she said, and caressed the weapon. "Is there a weapon that can kill every kind of monster and demon, I mean truly kill them?"

"There is. Not all of them are for a specific race, and not every weapon will always kill. I have some that will freeze or send others into panic. There are some that will kill a demon, but would do nothing more than irritate others. It's important to know what you are going to deal with, so you always bring the right tool for the job."

"Like don't bring a plunger to change a light bulb," she joked, but that was exactly what it was like. You don't bring a bag of cats to put out a fire. Well, that's a bad analogy. I might bring that. You can fight fire with all the evil that would be contained in a bag of cats.

We drove east along Wellesley Street after we were all set with goodies and drinks. The streets weren't as busy today. It might be because it was still Sunday night to many, or that it was nearly ten degrees colder than it had been the last time we were out. To kill the silence, I turned on the radio and dialed it over to a talk radio station. Of course, the talk of the town was the series of killings.

"So the police are combing the streets, looking for someone to pin these murders on, but have you seen a show of force out there on the street?" the radio personality asked, his voice rough and his pitch making him sound more like a carny barker than anything else. "I mean, every night on my drive home, I'm lucky if I see one cop car the entire time, and yet they claim they have people working overtime on the case. I call lies. The cops, they don't care about any of us. They're the ones who help fill the streets with drugs, and guns, and turn a blind eye when gangs kill each other. This is just par for the course."

"Can we turn that off?" Rouge asked, rolling her eyes and

groaning. "He sounds like a conspiracy guy. So many people do these days."

I reached over and switched it to a classic rock station, and found Pearl Jam singing about evolution. When did Pearl Jam become classic rock? They're not that old. Or are they? Sometimes, I feel as though time is passing by faster and faster every damn day.

"Have you noticed that?" Rouge asked, turning the volume down slightly.

"What? How anything older than ten years is classic rock?"

"No, not that. I mean how everyone acts as though everything in the world is a conspiracy. They don't like the way something is going, it must be something evil, hidden. You have people saying milk and water are turning people gay, that there are secret Satanic child trading rings under pizza shops with no basements, how their TVs are listening to them for the CIA. People think movies are being made to warp kids into becoming right-wingers, or left-wingers, that planes are spraying chemicals to kill people, and how aliens are actually government officials running experiments on their own people. Talk radio, social media, and the regular media are some of the worst things to ever happen to our society. Anything to get clicks, viewers, and shares."

"Wow," I said when she finally paused for a breath. "Have you been holding that in for a while?"

"Not really," she said, and blushed. "It's just when I see these things or hear them, I can't help but shake my head and wonder how long humans are going to survive on this planet."

"Humans?" I chuckled. "You almost make it sound like you're looking at them from the outside."

She paused and shrugged as she turned and looked out the window. "Maybe I am. Maybe I look at the people around us and just can't even relate to them anymore. Especially when I hear shit like that."

"See," I told her. "At least when we move to the country, we won't have to deal with all these so-called 'people'. But there is something to look at on the bright side."

"Really? What?"

"With all the focus on the murders right now, nobody is talking about me or calling me. I mean, sure, I've changed my phone number and that helped, but aside from those people at Sam's, nobody is really noticing me."

"I didn't, but now that you mention it, you're right. I haven't heard a single 'Yo, monster dude' for a while now. I guess that's something good we can take from this whole mess."

That was about the only thing good we could get out of this.

I turned onto Homewood Avenue, and headed south towards Allen Gardens. There were prostitutes everywhere along that particular stretch; all of them were transgender, which was why the area had the terrible nickname it did. We came to a stop at a stop sign and I looked west towards Church Street, wondering if we should head that way. As I looked, I saw someone I recognized and chuckled to myself.

"What is it?" Rouge asked, and I pointed towards a prostitute in a skirt much too short for the weather.

"That's Marvin!" I laughed, and drove over to where he was.

"I don't think you should do that," Rouge said.

"Do what?"

"Call her *Marvin*. It's kind of a dick thing to do."

"Why would it be a dick thing to do to call Marvin by his name?" I asked, very confused by it all.

"She's a trans woman, so I'm sure if she heard you calling her by that name, she'd be offended. It's rude."

I shook my head, and as we came to a stop I unrolled her window. "I wasn't talking about her. I'm talking about *him*."

"Hey, honeys," the woman said, leaning into the window, her Spanish accent as thick as the layer of perfume she wore. "I don't normally do couples, but for the right price, I will for you two."

"Not looking for fun," I said. "I'm here to talk to Marvin."

There was a moment where she tried to play it off like she had no idea what I was talking about, as though she'd never heard the name "Marvin" before. I hadn't seen Marvin in years, and had no idea what he'd been up to since our last run-in. Sometimes when you let monsters stay here, for whatever reason, you rarely check up on them to make sure they're behaving. I wouldn't have pictured this being the life he'd chose to live, but who was I to judge?

"Come on, Marvin," I said, looking the woman directly in the face. "It's been a long time, but not so long for me to forget you."

"You're not here to send me back, are you?" Marvin finally said, speaking up and catching Rouge off guard to the point where she let out a gasp. Maybe I should have prepared her for what she had been about to see, but it was funny to get her like that.

"No. I'm not here for you at all, Marvin. I'm looking at something bigger. Maybe you can help."

Rouge slowly leaned over to me. "Is that wig talking to us?" she asked, referring to the large, black, curly mass of hair sitting on the prostitute's head.

"That's not just any wig," I told her, as Marvin and the woman leaned closer towards the open window. "That there is Marvin, a Parzeek who I met about ten years ago in Sarnia."

"I try not to remember that time," Marvin said, but despite him not wanting to remember, I told Rouge about it.

I had gone to Sarnia over some strange reports of a monster there scaring people. What I found, instead, was a slaughter house. I arrived hours after someone or some*thing* walked into a diner and killed ten people who'd been there having breakfast. The murderer didn't shoot or stab them. The victims were all torn to pieces, ripped limb from limb. I met with the police, offered my help, and despite the fact that they didn't know who I was, or what I really did, word from the mayor of St. Catharine's got me into the crime scene to see what had happened.

There was blood and flesh everywhere. The walls were painted with people who'd had no idea their life would end in that grimy, poorly lit place. An eyeball lay on a plate with scrambled eggs, a human jaw in a bowl of porridge. And all over everything was *hair*.

I started to look around the town, and it wasn't long before I found Marvin and got ready to dispatch him. Yet, he seemed too weak, too frail to have wrought that sort of destruction, created such carnage. I questioned Marvin, a monster hidden in a wig belonging to an older woman who suffered from *alopecia areata*. He swore he hadn't done it, would never hurt a human, and made a deal with me that if I let him stay, he would help me solve the case.

He did help. Marvin led me to a young man, the type who was a born loser, and though he wasn't wearing a wig, another Parzeek had managed to somehow possess the mullet of this young man. I guess human hair is dead, so that was probably how it managed it.

The creature was mad, and wild, much stronger than I would have expected. I was lucky to get out of there in one piece, and when I did, I kept my promise to Marvin and didn't send him back to where he was from. In fact, I was so grateful for his help I did another favour for him, and brought him to the city. He hated Sarnia, said there was nothing to see there, and dreamed of life in Toronto being much more exciting.

"So is the city everything you hoped it would be, Marvin? I guess you see all sorts from up there."

"Hey now" the woman who housed Marvin on her head said. "There's nothing wrong with this kind of work. I help people who can't find love the way they want. I'm like a sex therapist for all the sad people who need me to give them comfort."

"I'm not judging. Just saying."

"Well, keep those comments in your pocket, and get on with why you're here. You're cramping business."

"No need to be rude, Cherry," Marvin said from on high. "Dillon here's a good one. What's bringing you around here?"

"Have you, either of you seen anything strange around here?"

"Oh honey, all we see around here is strange and unusual," Cherry laughed, adjusting her so-called skirt. It was more like a thin piece of cloth stretched over her ass, but I'm not judging. "You're going to have to be more specific than that."

"Have you seen anyone working around here that's new, and doesn't look quite right?" I asked, and there was a look on Cherry's face that told me everything.

"You're here looking for them? Good. They creep me the fuck

out, and if I never see them again, all the better. Wait," Cherry said, and looked excited about something. "Are those sisters like Marvin? Are they from space, too?"

"I'm not from space," Marvin said, sounding offended. "I'm from an actual planet."

"Whatever, girl," Cherry laughed, and continued talking to me. "Are they, you know, aliens too?"

"We think so," I told her. "You said *sisters?*"

"Yeah. There's three of them," Cherry said. "Some days they're together, other days it's just one or two of them. I haven't seen them in a few days, though."

This was perfect. We had one of them in the back seat, which meant there were only two more left. That was a start, a place to start from. First, though, I needed to know for sure if they were talking about the same thing, if the sisters were indeed the Chornak sex dolls. I reach behind us and pulled the sheet off to reveal the lifeless thing back there.

"Is this one of them?" I asked, and Cherry leaned in so she and Marvin could get a good look. She jumped back a second later and stepped away from the car.

"What did you do? My god!" She crossed herself and nearly took off, by the looks of it, but Marvin called out and calmed her down.

"It's not what you think, Cherry. Look again. That's metal showing underneath, not an actual skull." The wig, Marvin, shifted a little, turning to me in a comical way. "What was in it? Is it another Parzeek like me, like the one in that mullet?"

I shook my head as Cherry straightened her wig.

"No. These ones are Chornaks. You know what they are?" I asked.

"I don't, but are they the ones killing everyone around the city, cutting heads off people?" Marvin asked, and I nodded, told him they were actually *eating* the heads of their victims.

"Those sisters are eating Johns?" Cherry cried out and put a hand to her chest dramatically, and then started fanning herself. "What is this world coming to?"

"Do either of you know where they might be coming from? Where they're staying?"

Neither did, but Marvin did offer something to me.

"They always arrive by taxi. A Beck cab, number 6660," Marvin said. "Most of the ladies on the strip here come on foot, so when they arrived by cab, it's something you notice. The cab number also sticks in my head. I can't believe I never picked up that they weren't real people. In this light though, it's hard to tell, but I knew there was something not right about them."

"Yeah," Cherry said. "They walked weird, and their faces barely moved when they talked."

"Can you think of anything else about them or the cabbie?" Rouge asked, having been quiet for so long.

"Well, we do know the driver of the taxi," Marvin said, and Cherry agreed. "His name is Ali. He's the one who tends to drop them off, and later on picks them up, too. There are a lot of cabbies that do that kind of work, but if you're looking for those freaky sisters, you need to get a hold of him. I hope that helps."

"More than you know," I admitted. "You wouldn't by any chance have a phone number of this cab driver, would you?" I asked, and Cherry said "Of course," and gave it to us. I couldn't help but smile as I looked down at it.

"You might want to get this gorgeous lady here to call the number and tell Ali that you need a pickup. Not sure he ever picks boys up," Cherry offered, one last bit of help, and we exchanged our farewells. We drove off with our first real lead, and tried to figure out the best place to go to contact the cab driver and see if he could lead us to our prey.

We decided to go over to Parliament Street, head to a gas station which also had a *Tim Horton's* there so we could have some coffee and wait until the cabbie, Ali, arrived. Rouge called as we parked and gave him the address we wanted him to come to. He told her he'd be there in ten minutes, time enough to get our stuff. We sat in the Jeep, waiting for his arrival in relative silence for nearly two minutes.

"So, you fought a mullet once?" Rouge finally said, breaking the quiet between us.

"Yeah. Not the strangest thing I've ever fought, either," I admitted, and thought of the years and years I'd been on Earth and all the bizarre creatures I'd come in contact with.

"You're really going to have to tell me some of these stories," she laughed.

"Well, in all the free time we'll have when we move to the country, I will tell you one story every day. I may get through them all."

Just then, a cab with the number 6660 on the back end of it pulled in and parked.

"Here we go," I said, and we stepped out of the car and headed towards the cab.

The driver looked like nobody in particular. He was middle-aged, a little grey in the beard, and seemed to have a small-framed body. He didn't notice us at all. His phone was in his hand and he was no doubt about to call the number Rouge used to call him when I knocked on the window. He turned, looked at me and then at Rouge, before he slowly rolled down his window with a confused look on his face.

"I'm off duty," he said, even though I knew he wasn't. "Go find another cab. I don't have time for you."

"Is that because you're here to pick up a working girl?" I asked, and those words certainly got his attention. Things were going to go one of two ways, as far as I could see. He was either going to run, or be so afraid that we were cops and he was about to be taken in that he would break down and cry, weep a confession to us. He paused, his lips quivering, and I knew it was going to be the latter. I opened the back door of the cab and both of us stepped inside. "Don't worry, Ali. We're not the cops."

"So, you're here to rob me?" he asked, his voice still shaky as he stared at us in the rear-view mirror.

"No," Rouge said gently, and put a hand on his shoulder. "It's nothing like that. We just need to know about some people you give rides to, where they might live."

"Please," he begged and shook his head, and I wondered what he was afraid of. Was it the women who had a secret on him, that they offered their bodies for rides and someone close to him like a wife might find out? Or was it that some of the women might have pimps and he feared repercussions? "If I tell you, nobody will trust me, or call me ever again. Driving this cab doesn't make close to enough money to live in this city. These people I help out are the only way I can survive."

It had to be more than that, but I didn't want to push it.

"I'm sure you won't have any problems with these ones," Rouge said, still keeping her hand on his shoulder. "It's three sisters. A little strange looking and—"

"Oh! Them?" Ali asked, and turned in his seat to look at us. "I don't mind telling you about them. There's something I don't like about those three."

"I'm sure," Rouge said, and nodded. "We just want to know if you pick them up or drop them off at the same place each time. Possibly if you might know where they live?"

He shook his head. "I don't know where they live, but I have picked them up and dropped them off at the same spot many times."

"Can you take us there? Or just tell us where it is?"

He didn't want to take us, but he did point us in the right direction.

We were so close to shutting the book on this case.

Ali didn't know exactly where the sisters went to when they left his cab, or where they came from when he picked them up, but he did say that whenever he did either, it was always from the same corner in Bloor West Village. He said they were always on the north side of Windermere Avenue, but as we pulled up and parked, we realized there were so many places these two might be that it would be like looking for a needle in a haystack. Bakeries, butchers, a few clothing stores, a drug store, a toy store, two book stores, and each store had an apartment overhead. Not only that, but there were side streets all over the place full of homes where the sisters could be. There was also a medical facility, a church with a funeral parlour attached to it, and a ton of restaurants and specialty stores. There was nothing as obvious as a sign that said *WE SELL SEX DOLLS* to tell us where to find them.

"So," Rouge said, eyeing the streets outside of the Jeep. "Where do we even start?"

"I have no idea," I admitted. "They could be anywhere. All we can do is sit here and wait for them to show up, I guess."

"Oh, this is going to be fun," she joked, and poked me in the ribs. "Hope you're not going to be sneaking stinkers out like you were when we were driving around earlier."

"I did no such thing," I scoffed. "I'm a lady, and ladies don't fart."

"Yeah right," she laughed. "When you sleep, you don't snore, your ass does."

"If I don't hear it, it never happened," I said, but felt a sudden gurgling in my stomach. I had been letting out some bad ones before we ran into Marvin, but that was because I clearly needed to use the washroom. "I think I need to make a run for the *Pizza Pizza* over there. Are you going to be okay in here?"

"Aside from the creepy dead doll in the back seat, I'll be fine. Just make sure your cellphone is on in case one or both of them come back."

I pulled out my phone and checked it, and sure enough it was set on *DO NOT DISTURB*. I quickly turned it back to vibrate mode and asked her if she wanted anything while I was gone. She asked me to bring her back something delicious and cheesy.

"So, just bring myself back, got it," I joked, and moved as fast as I could to the store

I walked in and asked where the bathroom was, and the man behind the counter looked me up and down with a scowl on his face.

"Washrooms are for customers only," he told me.

"I'm going to buy something when I'm done."

"No. You buy first, and then I'll give you the key."

"Fine," I conceded, and ordered two slices and two drinks. Even after I paid, he was still reluctant to hand over the key, but when he did, I saw it was for the women's restroom. "Uh, I think you gave me the wrong key."

"No. It's the right one. Men's is in use. You want the toilet, you use the women's. Man been in there for a long time, but he is regular customer, so he can take as long as he likes. You want the key or no?"

"Sure," I said, and took it from him. I had to go, and I didn't want to wait to use a bathroom some guy was no doubt killing at the moment. I headed there, not ashamed to use the women's washroom at all, and shot a look over at the men's room. It didn't smell horrible, but the guy was making a lot of noise, so this was probably for the best.

At least it didn't take long and the washroom was clean. I washed my hands in the sink, dried them off with a powerful hand dryer and headed out with key in hand to get my food. I stopped the second I got out and nearly pulled my Tincher from my belt. My eyes went up to the corner of the hall I was in and saw a camera there. I couldn't pull it out and risk getting caught, but there was clearly something wrong in there.

From the bottom of the door, I could see blood. I realized one of the sisters must be in there with the regular customer who'd gone into the bathroom, and he was having his head eaten. The sounds I'd heard and thought was someone shitting were clearly those of a Chornak chowing down.

What now?

Call Rouge? Call Garcia? Or do what I do and kick the door in and go toe-to-toe with a monster?

There was no time to do anything but fight. I couldn't allow this thing to get away. I grasped the handle of my blade, took a step back, and kicked the door as hard as I could. I'd done it so many times before, booting in doors to someone's house, a garage, but never in a pizza place. And that would be why I bounced back, a bolt of pain flying up my leg, the door still in place.

"Shit," I whispered. It was a metal door in a metal frame. There was no way I was kicking the damn thing open. I grabbed my leg, and thought about kicking it again so it didn't suddenly fly open and the monster in there come out charging after me. Before I could, though, the other door, the one I had come in through, flew wide.

"What the fuck are you doing?" the employee who took my order yelled. "Why you kicking the door? You a druggie?"

"No," I said, and pointed to the floor. "Look!"

His eyes followed, and he cursed under his breath. He dug in his pocket and came out with a set of keys and walked over to unlock the men's washroom. I had no idea what to do. If he opened it and saw one of the sisters in there, he'd freak out. He might even get killed in the process. I couldn't let that happen, but I wasn't sure how to explain it to him, either.

"Let me do it," I offered, and held my hand out. "Just in case it's a huge mess he made, you shouldn't have to get messy."

He looked at me like I was crazy, because what I'd said made no real sense. Why should I care if he got messy? Why hadn't I thought of something better than that?

"Just move. I have to see what's going on in there." He moved to the door and banged on it. "Hey in there, are you okay? What are you doing in there?" There was no answer, and he knocked louder. "If you don't say something, I'm coming in there." Again, there was only silence. The employee cursed under his breath and put the key in the door. He paused a moment, took in a deep breath and pushed the door open. I was at his side, ready to do whatever I had to in order to ensure the monster didn't get out of there alive.

The smell of blood was the first thing to hit me, but as I looked inside, and the carnage in there, the smell of shit soon followed.

"What is this?" the employee gasped, staring at the scene before us. "What did you do to him?" he asked, and turned to me.

"What the hell are you talking about?" I said, letting go of my Tincher and moving away from the door. I'd seen enough. The man hadn't been eaten by a Chornak at all.

"Look at him!" the employee said and pointed into the bathroom. "How could that happen? You did something?"

"That's not my area of expertise. I'm sure EMS or the coroner will be able to figure it out, but if you don't believe me, check your cameras."

"But what am I supposed to do with this mess?"

"Start by calling 911," I suggested, and decided to make my exit. There was nothing for me to do. I guess it would've been just too easy if one or both of the sisters had been in the washroom with the dead man. I'm sure the employee would have noticed a woman, especially one who looked like a living sex doll, and would've made her buy something before going into the washrooms.

I made my way out as the man went to the counter and dialed for help. The air was crisp and smelled so much better than it had in the store, especially the washroom. I shook my head and tried to get it back in the game, wanting to be ready for what came next. My heart was still moving at a rapid rate from the fight I had been expecting.

Halfway to the Jeep, ready to tell Rouge the story of what had just happened, I realized I'd forgotten the food. I turned back to *Pizza Pizza,* wondering if I should even bother, but thought it was better to return with food and a story than just food.

The employee was as happy to see me as he had been the first time. He asked me what I wanted, and when I told him I was there for the food and pop I'd paid for, he looked at me as though I was disgusting. I guess he expected me to have lost my appetite. He was wrong.

Taking my order, I left the store and headed to the Jeep, but as I stepped back out into the brisk night, I saw someone standing by the car, looking into the rear driver's side window.

"Shit!"

I knew the woman, dressed like a movie hooker, was not just a woman. Even from the distance I was, I could see the way her skin looked under the orange glow of the street lamps, and there was nothing natural about it. I could see how it had to be one of the sisters from here, so how come Rouge hadn't noticed? Squinting through the dark street, I could see the shape of Rouge still in the front seat on the passenger's side. I could see the glow of her cellphone on her face. She must've been too busy scrolling through websites to notice the monster we were hunting was right there.

I had to do something, and fast.

I tossed the food and drinks into the trash can beside me, and pulled my cellphone out as I circled around the Jeep to stay out of the sister's sightline, just in case she looked over. I dialed Rouge and she answered on the second ring.

"You're taking a while," she scoffed. "Are you almost done, I'm—"

"I need you to listen to me," I said, cutting her off, but not wanting her to panic and get into a fight with the creature. Not until I got there, at least. "I found one of the sisters, but whatever you do, do not move, or even look around to see."

"What? Where is she?"

"Keep your voice down and don't move. I'm on my way."

"On your way?" she asked, and I could hear her voice waver. "She's here, isn't she? At the car?"

"I'm coming, Rouge. Just stay there."

"Oh shit. Why did you have to tell me? I was just looking at shoes, and you had to tell me this! And now you expect me not to freak out or even move? You better hurry then," she whispered and I was doing just that.

I hung up, closing the gap on the Jeep and the sister beside it. I pulled my Tincher out, knowing I was in open view of the public, but not caring. There weren't many people around, but also because I had the monster in my sights and knew I had to act fast for both our sakes.

As I moved closer, the urge to run at her grew, but I didn't want to call any attention to myself. I could hear the sex doll sister was saying something. She repeated the words "What have they done to you, sister?" as she looked into the Jeep where the covered body her kin once lived in lay. I wasn't sure how she knew the body was there, what made her be able to sense it, but in the end it didn't matter. She had, and now we had snared this one in an unintended trap.

I managed to make it to the rear of the Jeep, unseen and unnoticed. In the distance, I could hear the sound of sirens, no doubt for the call about the dead man in the bathroom at *Pizza Pizza*. It's funny how I thought I was about to catch one of the sisters there, but instead she'd found us. And with the emergency vehicles on the way, I didn't have time to waste. I didn't want to be in a fight with a silicone doll when police, fire department, or EMS showed up. I had to move, and now.

I took a deep breath, calmed my adrenaline-filled limbs and gripped my Tincher tightly. I moved around the Jeep, ready for a sneak attack, but she realised I was coming and as I turned the corner we were face to face with one another. Her glass eyes stared at me, her face stuck in a motionless state of sexual desire, but I could sense the anger in her the second before she charged at me.

"Murderer!" she screamed, and had her hands on me before I could take a step back. She was strong, her grip like steel as she grabbed my coat and threw me against the Jeep. I fought back, raising the Tincher up to her throat and pressing the blade to it. I didn't want to cut her or send her out of the body she was in just yet. I wanted answers. I needed to know where her other sister was, and how they had gotten into those bodies, where the weak spot was, but the blade did little to stop her rage. She struck out at the hand holding the Tincher, hitting it with enough force that it flew from my hand, but not before it took a chunk of her jawbone off. "You think you can kill me with your little toy?" she growled with her motionless face. "You think I'm as weak as my sister? Your blade is useless."

"What about this?" Rouge said from our side, the Thurkk in her hand, raised to strike. I went to tell her *no*, to stop her before she could do anything, but was too late.

The point of the curved spike pierced the chest of the sister and a sound escaped the monster like the air being let out of a balloon. The hands that held me fell away as blue light came out of the doll's eyes and mouth in the form of a mist, seconds before it fell backwards, the Thurkk pulling free of it.

"Well, that was easy," Rouge said, and she was smiling as she looked down at the dead, lifeless doll. It was dead, more so than the one in the back of the car because of the weapon used. My Tincher would have simply sent the essence that was within the doll back to the planet it came from. The Thurkk, on the other hand, had snuffed the monster out of existence completely, giving her a true death.

But Rouge was right. It was easy, only now it would make things harder because we still had one sister on the loose. If we had captured this one, we might've had a key into finding the other; now we had to do it on our own.

"Are those for us?" Rouge said, pointing to the approaching lights, the sirens now even closer.

"No, but we need to pick her up and get her in the car," I said, indicating to the doll. "I'll explain why they're here later. Give me a hand."

After we packed the body on top of the other one, we got back into the Jeep. We managed to do it all before the first emergency vehicle showed up in front of the pizza place. I was worn out and tired from the effort, and from the day itself. I didn't start the car, or drive away right away. Instead, I simply stared out the window, looking at nothing in particular as I thought about what a wasted opportunity we'd just had slip through our fingers.

"So, what's with all the sirens?" Rouge asked, turning in her seat to look at what was going on. "They're going to *Pizza Pizza*. What happened in there?"

"Nothing really," I said, barely paying attention to her.

"Dillon? What's wrong?"

"Oh, nothing," I tried to lie, but knew she wasn't going to buy it. "It's just, we had a chance to get something out of her, to find out where her sister was, or even where they'd come from."

"Well, at least we have bait, right?"

"Bait?"

"Yeah. I mean, clearly this one I just killed was somehow drawn to the body of the other one. Can't we use that to catch the last sister?"

"Maybe. We can at least hope," I told her, and we drove off. I didn't want to be there when the police arrived. We'd just have to wait and figure out what came next.

Tuesday

We spent the night at Rouge's house. We thought about going to pick up the puppy, but decided it was better to let the little one stay with Sue until things settled and we were done with all this. I knew Rouge must miss her little fur baby, but there was no point in running back and forth and risking the little thing getting hurt. She called Sue and told her, and the two of us went to bed that night and slept in longer than I had in a while.

The best part about waking up that morning was checking the news on my phone and seeing there were no new bodies to report on. The city had been quieter last night, and I thought we'd had some sort of part in that. It was a little thing to hold onto, to give me hope of closing the case and moving on to leaving.

I turned over in bed after closing CP24's website, and found Rouge was gone. I went to the bedroom door and opened it, greeted by the smell of bacon cooking and coffee brewing. Heading downstairs, I could hear she was listening to some music and singing along. I stood in the doorway of the kitchen, watching her bobbing with the beat of the Si Cranstoun. She looked adorable doing it as she fried bacon and scrambled eggs.

She spun around in time with the song, and made a little squeak sound as she saw me there.

"How long have you been there?" she asked, blushing and turning back to the food.

"Long enough to think you're the cutest thing ever," I admitted, smiling. I had already put the defeat I felt after last night behind us. "How long have you been up?"

"Not too long, but I didn't want to disturb you so I thought I would come down and make some food for us. Did you sleep well?"

"Well enough. You see the news?"

"No. I don't internet until at least noon. The web is like booze. It's just not something you should do first thing in the morning. Why? Did something happen?"

"No. That's just it. Nothing happened at all," I told her, explaining there was nothing on the news about headless bodies being found anywhere.

"Well, that's a good thing then. We at least stopped it for a night. And we'll find the last sister. I'm sure of it. Then we can get a move on from all of *this*, right?"

I nodded and sat down while she finished cooking. I offered to help, but she told me to sit down, that she was almost done. She said I could wash the dishes though, and make lunch if I wanted to be useful. I guess that was fair enough.

We ate in relative silence. The food hit the spot, making me feel better with each salty bite. Afterwards, we went and sat out in the back yard and finished our coffees. The day was a bit warm, but the wind carried the scent of fireplaces to us. It was quiet and peaceful, a peek into the lives we would take hold of and enjoy the hell out of. I knew I'd love it, and I could only hope she would, too.

Serenity was interrupted, though, twenty minutes later when my phone vibrated and I saw it was Garcia calling. My stomach dropped for a second, ready to hear that they'd found another body after all. As it turned out, it was something else entirely.

"I didn't wake you, did I?" he asked when I answered. I told him no, that we'd been up and about for a while. "How did everything go last night?"

I told him that we'd found out a lot. I explained that there had been three of them all together, and that two were now dealt with, their bodies in the Jeep. He sounded relieved, that is until he said there was another problem. Isn't there always? I asked him what it was, and he told me he needed me to see it instead.

"How soon can you come down to 52 Division?"

"We could be there in half an hour," I told him. Rouge asked me what the call was about; I covered the mouthpiece and told her I had no idea, but Garcia wanted us to come see him. I had to assume he wasn't just wasting my time. "Does this have anything to do with the murders?" I asked.

"No. This has to do with the woman we brought in for stabbing you," he told me. Over the last two days, I hadn't thought about her—or the stabbing—even once. It was strange how something so painful could slip my mind.

"I'd totally forgotten about her. Do you need me to sign some sort of papers about it?"

"No. I need you here for something else, something a little stranger than simply signing paperwork."

"Is this something that can wait?" I asked, not sure I wanted to deal with all that at the moment.

"Not really," he said, and sounded tired. "There's only so long I can keep this as quiet as I already have. I'm also pretty sure this is not something you want to ignore."

I told him I'd be there and hung up. Rouge was still standing close by and I told her what Garcia had said. It was strange how easily I'd forgotten about that other woman I have a bad habit of letting things fall away from my thoughts when there's something bigger in my life. I rubbed the place where she had stabbed me, a woman I didn't know: nor had I any idea of why she'd done it. I'd been too busy with trying to heal, dealing with Parks and then the sisters, to even bother with the questions the woman's attack brought up.

"Should we head there right away?" Rouge asked, and I shrugged. I guessed we'd better. I was too interested in knowing what all this could be about.

We pulled up the station not long after hanging up the phone. Garcia stood out by the parking area, waiting for me and drinking coffee. As I stepped out of the car, he was right beside me, clearly anxious to talk.

"Thanks for showing up so quickly," he said, and turned towards Rouge. "I hope he's not dragging you into all the madness of his life."

"No, not dragging me. I go willingly to it," she said and smiled at us. "So, what's going on now? There's seems to be nothing but craziness following us at every turn."

"Well, get ready for a little more," he said, and leaned against the Jeep. "I was called in on this because I was the one who signed off on the arrest and took over the case to keep your name and information out of this. Now, it seems, I have no choice but to have us all involved."

"That certainly sounds ominous," I admitted.

"How well do you know the woman who was picked up?" Garcia asked.

"I don't know her at all. I thought Parks had sent her," I lied. In actuality, I had thought she *was* Parks, his soul in a new body come to kill me. I'd clearly been wrong about that. "Does she claim to know me?"

"Not really," he said, and went on to explain the story of what had happened since she was brought in on Friday.

When she was taken into custody, they took her to St. Michael's first as she had a bad wound to her head. She was slow waking up, no identification on her. When she finally came to, she began to rave like a maniac. She had to be strapped down, calling out for me, saying she wanted the monster hunter, and was moved from the emergency ward up to the mental health unit. There she had been medicated and eventually transferred over to the holding cells in 52 Division. Garcia hadn't seen her right away. He was still too busy with the case of the sisters eating people's heads, but another officer in Missing Persons saw her and recognized her from a report, giving Garcia a call as well as the woman's husband.

A report had been filed a week prior on her. Her husband had waited the mandatory twenty-four hours before contacting police, but nobody really looked into it. Garcia explained in cases like that, people assumed the wife had just packed up and left, figuring there'd been some sort of abuse or cheating going on.

The police would put out a notice on their website, but never bothered with any real investigation. It wouldn't be until a body showed up that they would bother with the report of a middle-aged adult.

Yet, one detective saw her at the station and recognized her from the report. He called Garcia and asked about her. Garcia told him what he could, leaving me out, and the two detectives met. Hours later, the woman's husband showed up, and the two were reunited. Only it wasn't the reunion they were expecting.

"The woman looked at her husband as though she'd never seen him before, asked if he was with the monster hunter or the Maker," Garcia said and shook his head. "Her husband said who he was, asked what had happened to her, and she turned away from the man, who was by then near tears and looked right at me. 'Bring me the monster hunter' she said, and I looked in her eyes. There was nothing in there even slightly kind or gentle. She looked as mad as any person I'd ever seen having a psychotic episode."

He went on, telling us how the man reached across the table, tried to take the hands of his wife, but she moved back in her seat and told him to leave, to get out or he'd regret it. She demanded to be taken back to her cell and despite his insistence on staying with her, she was led away and the detective had a lot of questions for Garcia.

"I could only tell him so much," Garcia admitted. "If I told him the whole story, can you imagine what he'd have thought? He might've even sent me to the hospital to get checked out as well."

"Is she still here?" I asked.

"She is, and that's the problem. Her husband came back yesterday while I was out at Police Headquarters over on College. He demanded to see his wife, but since there was no real paperwork on her, nothing filled out with any actual charges or victim or a crime, the desk sergeant decided to discharge her into his care."

"Then how is she still here?" Rouge said. "Did she come back after leaving, hoping Dillon would come to see her?"

"Not quite," he said, and drained the last of his coffee.

He only had the police report to go on. Her husband had

picked her up and drove her home. At the time, she had just been given the medication prescribed by the hospital, so she was very subdued. Four hours later, police dispatch received a call via 911 of a domestic dispute in the apartment the couple shared. Police arrived and entered the unit with the help of building security, after knocking on the door for several minutes. I listened to the story Garcia was telling us, feeling coldness in my stomach, because I could see this wasn't going to end well. Something terrible had happened.

"The officers on scene said they could hear crying coming from the bathroom. When they called out, there was no answer, so they cautiously headed over there and found the husband lying on the floor, half dead, in a pool of blood. He couldn't talk, but later we found out his wife had attacked him, knocked him to the ground and bit him several times. One of those bites was to the throat, where she took a huge chuck of skin with it, nicking his jugular vein."

"Jesus," Rouge gasped, and I nodded in agreement. "Is he okay, or did he die?"

"He's in stable condition, but he's going to have a hard time recovering mentally from it all," Garcia told us, and looked down at his feet.

"Where was the wife? How did your officers find her?" Rouge asked before I could.

"She hadn't left the apartment. She was in the bedroom, naked, covered in her husband's blood and eating stuff from their cat's litter box, of all things."

"Ew!" Rouge gasped and shook her head. "Then shouldn't she be back in the hospital? She's clearly sick."

I shook my head. "You said she was eating litter?"

"Yeah."

"Was it the shit, or piss?" I asked, knowing it was a weird thing to ask, but I was willing to put money on the fact that it was going to be the latter.

"The report didn't say. Why?"

"Is there a strange smell coming off her at all? Something like sulfur or ammonia?"

"She does smell a little off; a bit like spoiled milk and meat, with a hint of something chemical. You have some idea of what this is?"

I nodded and opened the car door, and grabbed my bag. I was going to need three items, but I wasn't positive they were in there, or sitting in my apartment. Luckily, I had them all. I couldn't be one hundred percent sure of what this was, but putting it all together, it led me to believe there was the work of a demon involved here. If I was right, it made a lot more sense why the woman had attacked me. I wasn't wrong thinking it was Parks after all. But I'd just let it go, relieved when it seemed he wasn't involved –but that was a mistake.

"Can I have access to her?" I asked, taking a piece of Yahudan glass and an Ephesian coin from my bag and putting it in my pocket. I continued to look through my bag, trying to see if I had a brass jar or tube. It had to be brass, but I wasn't sure I'd bothered to pack any of the vials I had which contained fluids, powders or potions.

"Of course you can see her," Garcia said as I shifted things around. "It's part of the reason I called you. I hope you know what this is all about, because I'm being asked a lot of questions about her now, and about you."

"I will do my best to help out," I said, and finally I found something that would work. It was a pear-shaped brass jar, and when I took the cork lid off I saw that all it held was water, which I could only assume had been blessed. Holy water came in handy on some occasions, but it would be easy to get more, so I dumped it out and pocketed the three items. After that we walked to the building.

"You care to share with the rest of the class?" Rouge asked.

"I can't be certain, but the more I hear, the more it makes sense to me," I explained. Garcia told us to wait in the front lobby while he went to get the woman out of her cell. I told him to make sure she was cuffed when she was put in one of the interview rooms, and he said of course he would. "I think the woman is possessed by a demon," I explained.

"A demon? Like the thing in Niagara Falls?"

"No. This sounds more like a demon who would normally attach itself to a human soul. Think of *The Exorcist,* if it helps."

"Can you do anything to help her?"

"If that's what we're dealing with, then yes I can. They can be nasty as anything else, but if she's cuffed, then we should have no problem."

A few minutes later, Garcia came back and was shaking his head.

"Is everything okay?" I asked, sure for a second that he hadn't been able to bring her out of her cell.

"She doesn't look the same," he whispered, and led us down the hall. "I saw her only two days ago and she was fine, but now she looks sunken in and starved, like someone dying."

That was a clear sign of possession.

"She's in Interrogation Room number three. I'm not going to come in with you, if you don't mind," Garcia said, and looked at the door with something close to fear in his eyes. "I'll stay out here, to keep an eye on the room to make sure nobody comes in. Cameras and microphones will also be turned off."

I thanked him, and then I walked into the room with Rouge at my side. The first thing I noticed, aside from the sight of the woman hunched over the table, was the smell. It was a mix of salty sea water, sulfur, and human sweat. There was little reason to doubt there was a demon involved in this mess. Demons always have a smell about them, and that smell is always foul, one way or another.

I shut the door, and when I did, the woman looked up at us. She looked small and frail at first, but as soon as her eyes met my face, a change happened. Her own face darkened, eyes narrowed, and her mouth twisted into a grimace of hate and pain. She knew me. Whatever was inside her knew who I was, and not just because she had stabbed me.

"You came, hunter," she growled and tried to get up, but she was handcuffed to the table. "Get these things off of me so I can put my hands on you again."

"I don't think so," I said, and leaned against the wall.

"It felt so good to sink that knife into you. I would have bit into you, too, if your whore friend hadn't stopped me," she said, and looked at Rouge. "I can't wait to get my hands on you too, maggot."

"You won't get the chance," Rouge said, and sat down on one of the two chairs across from the possessed woman. "Why don't you tell us who you really are?"

"He should know," the demon said with the woman's mouth. "You remember me, don't you, monster hunter. We met not that long ago."

I shrugged. "All you demons look and smell alike," I said and reached into my pocket, where I found the Yahudan glass; I raised it to my right eye. Looking through it, the room darkened, as it always does, and when I turned my gaze onto the woman at the table, I saw through her flesh, past the human to the demon cancer inside. The creature was small, and thin, its skin was more like cracked rocks than meat. It smiled at me from within, knowing I was seeing its true form, and knew I had to recognize it.

"How did you find your way back here, Golooth?" I asked still looking through the glass as I sat beside Rouge.

"So, you do remember me?"

"How could I forget the dumbest Gorno I ever met," I said and laughed at the demon, wanting to make it angry, hoping to get it would give me what I wanted. "I can't believe you would try and come here again after I sent you back to the hellhole of a home you came from. Being ripped out and sent back wasn't good enough once, you wanted to come back and be made a fool of again?"

"It's different this time, hunter," the demon cackled, and struggled against the cuffs again. "You'll regret casting me out this time."

"And why's that? You have something hidden away that will cause me some sort of pain?"

"Not just you. You have no idea what you're dealing with this time, hunter. The seas of change are here. I am only one in the many."

"Can you just shut him up?" Rouge asked, and I was tempted

to just be done with it, too.

"Careful or I will shut you up, thief," the demon said, turning to look at Rouge. "I can smell the stain on you, whore; you stupid little pretender. He might not, but I do, and I would watch that foul tongue before it gets eaten."

"Enough of this," I said, standing up and putting the glass back in my pocket. I exchanged it for the coin and held it in front of the demon to see.

"You can't do this, hunter. It isn't like the last time. Send me out and the woman will surely die."

I shook my head and walked over to the woman with the beast inside her. The smell coming off it grew as the fear beat through the demon within. I had heard creatures beg before, just as I had heard others threaten harm would come to someone if I banished them back to where they came from. I knew those threats to be nothing more than words. They were just the impotent ultimatums of some monster afraid of being removed from this world.

"Nothing will happen to her, just as nothing happened to the last man you inhabited," I said, and moved the coin towards the woman's head.

"Don't do it, hunter. I'm telling you, this is different. You have no idea how I came here, how I found this woman," he pleaded, but I wasn't listening. There was no point in hearing out the damned thing. Every word, every breath, was fouled with lies and deceits. "If you kill me now, you'll never know how to find the s—"

The words died on the woman's lips as the coin touched her head. It was amazing to watch it work. The woman went into a small seizure, fists tightening into balls and black smoke bleeding from her eyes, mouth and nose. Inside, the demon made a sound, like someone gargling water. This was it being ripped from the woman. It was being pulled out and would have been propelled back to its hell world, if not for the fact that I'd pulled the brass bottle out and drew the mist into it. It took all of ten seconds, and the woman fell still, before she slumped forward, face against the table. I corked the bottle and smiled at Rouge. I'm sure the

Catholic church would love these little gifts instead of just using holy water and scripture.

"Easier than anything else we've done lately," I said, and I took out the glass again. I pressed it against my eye and saw no sign of the demon.

She was free of it, safe from the demon that was now trapped in the jar.

"What are you going to do with that?" she asked, and pointed over to the jar.

"Normally I would just send it back, but I think it deserves a better punishment than that. After stabbing me and messing with this woman and her husband, I can think of a few choice ways to handle it."

"What about her? Is she going to be okay?" Rouge asked, looking at the motionless woman.

"She will be. She's just unconscious from the ordeal. This kind of thing happens more than three quarters of the time." I leaned down and checked the woman's pulse. It was very shallow, and that wasn't normal at all. Usually people tended to have a rapid heartbeat from the exorcism of the demon. I was sure she was going to be fine though, and checked her pupils as well. I opened her left eyelid and pulled my cellphone out. I shone the light in her eye, but nothing happened; no dilation at all.

Shit.

That couldn't be good.

"What's wrong?" Rouge asked, no doubt sensing my worry. "Is she okay?"

"I don't know. Her heart rate is low, and her pupils are static. I've never seen this before."

"Is there something you can do to help her?"

"I don't even know what's wrong with her, Rouge. I've never seen this before and I don't like it one bit."

I shook the woman, tapped her cheek, but there was no reaction whatsoever. I took her pulse again, and it seemed way too slow. I pulled out a safety pin from my pocket—lucky I had one—and poked the woman's right index finger with it, gently, but hard enough to draw blood. No reaction at all.

This was not good.

I went over to the door, opened it and called Garcia in. When he entered, his eyes went right to the woman head down on the table, and asked what was wrong. I told him what had happened, and what the situation was. He wanted to know what it meant, and I wished I could've given him an answer.

"This is not going to go well for me, Dillon. I'm the one who brought her here, shut off the camera, and now she's like this. What am I supposed to say?"

"I don't know," I admitted, and looked at that the still woman. Had I made a mistake removing the demon? It had warned me not to, but I'd just assumed it was an idle threat. Demons were infamous for telling lies, so why would I think this was any different? I could hear Garcia muttering to himself as he opened the door of the interview room and scanned the hallway.

"We're going to have to come up with something, and fast. I can't let anyone see us in here like this. It'll be hard enough for me to explain what happened to her, never mind why you two are here with her."

"Dillon," Rouge said, and put her hand on my shoulder and gave it a squeeze. "Is there any way to put the demon back into her for now until you figure this out? It'll at least save problems for Garcia."

"I could," I said, though I didn't like the idea. Who knew what the demon would do to her now that it knew we were aware of it? Demons are not the nicest or most forgiving of creatures I deal with. In fact, they tend to be the very worst and most vile, never ones to shy away from the pain or death of a person, even if that person is the host body. I could only imagine how this must be for the woman who was unconscious, but as I tried to put myself in her place I had an idea that it was exactly what I needed to do. "I have an idea," I said, and looked over at Garcia. "You might not like it, though. Either of you."

I told them my plan and I was right: they hated the idea.

"You can't do that," Rouge said, almost pleading with me after I explained that I was going to open the vial and drink the demon into me. The hope was that once it was inside, I would be able to get the upper hand and I could force answers from the damned thing. I'd never done anything like this before—having a spiritual fight with a monster—but there was a first time for everything. "How do you know you'll be okay? What if you end up like her, or worse?"

"Can you think of a better plan?" I asked, and when she didn't answer I turned to Garcia. "I'm going to need you to put handcuffs on me. I don't want this demon to get the upper hand and make me hurt myself for real."

"Oh, this sounds so much better than what we already have to deal with," Garcia said, his voice thick with sarcasm. "You really think this will do anything?"

"I have to try. Look at her. I can't think of anything else. I need answers to what he did to her."

"Rouge is right, though. There's a chance you could end up like her, too. What if that happens?"

"It won't, but if it does, I'll just..." I stopped there before I could finish my thought. What I wanted to say was I would leave this body and move to another, but I didn't need Garcia to freak out even more over the whole situation. He still didn't know everything about me, after all. Some things were just harder for humans to swallow. "You know no matter what, I'll be fine, right, Rouge?"

She didn't look so sure, but nodded anyway.

"I need your help, too," I told her as I was cuffed to the table along with the unconscious woman. "I need you to pour the demon into my mouth."

"Don't put this on me," she whispered, and stepped away from the table.

"This is the life you want to be a part of, Rouge, so I need you to help."

"Fine," she said, but there was no way she sounded okay with it. Still, I needed her to be part of this, and if she really wanted to be a hunter, there would always be choices we'd have to make that she wouldn't be happy with. "Anything else?"

"Yes. Use the glass and the coin. The glass will help you see that the demon is in me. The coin will pull it from me when the work is done, but don't let the mist get away. I need you to catch it in that brass bottle the way I did."

"And how will I know the job is done? How am I supposed to know when to use the coin?"

"I will say a word, something off topic. You'll know it when you hear it."

"Why not just say it now?"

"Because there's a chance Golooth is listening. Now, is everyone ready for this?"

If you've never been possessed by a demon, you might not know how shocking it is when you feel the cold darkness slowly bleed into you. At first, you notice it in your hands and feet, but slowly the icy sensation fills you up and your brain is set ablaze with a sub-zero fire. Your bones feel as though they will shatter, your joints stiffen and crack if you try to move. It was a kind of torture I didn't want to endure, but there was no other choice. And this wasn't the first time my body had been invaded by outside forces, but as I sat at the table, having Golooth move through the same body as I was in, I hoped this might be the last.

I closed my eyes, relaxed as best I could. I ignored the pain and waited for it to try to take control of my body. I was expecting to just fight against the presence of it, to weaken him and squeeze the answers I need from the demon, but instead I could see the creature.

Behind my closed lids, the grey, stone-like body of the Gorno stepped out of the shadows and stared right at me.

"What is going on here, hunter?" Golooth asked and took a step back, nearly disappearing into the shadows again. "Where are we?"

"You're here, with me, inside my body," I told him as I moved in his direction. "You're going to tell me what you did to that woman, and how I can get her back to normal."

"I told you not to remove me, hunter. I warned you, but you don't listen. You hunters are all the same, never hearing anything other than what you want."

"So tell me now. Explain what's wrong with her. Why isn't she responsive?"

"Why should I tell you anything, hunter? So you can lock me away again, or send me back to the stinking rivers of shit I'm forced to live by? Why don't I just deal with you and keep your body for myself?"

"Because you'd never win."

"Wouldn't I? You have no weapons here. You have no blessed items that can paralyze me, or send me out of you suddenly."

"You're right, I don't," I admitted.

"Then, you're mine," he growled, and charged at me. In normal circumstances, I might've run, or at least tried to fight back, but I knew something he didn't. I'm always prepared, even when my hands appear empty.

The demon's hands went straight for my throat. They were cold, and as hard as the stone they looked like, but as they touched, even before it could squeeze them together, Golooth cried out and fell backwards. His spirit body hit the metaphysical ground as his hands, which had been steel grey, turned black.

"What did you do to me?" he cried out, still looking at the smoldering fingers he'd used to try and strangle the life from me.

"I might not have a weapon in my hand, demon, but that doesn't mean I'm not armed. You didn't ever think you're not fighting the real me, the physical form of Dillon. You're inside my body, a body covered in tattoos which protect me from low level demon shits like you. I think what you felt was the *Eye of Raamaathaa*. You want to try again?"

The demon didn't make another move on me, though he might've been trying to figure out how he could. I approached the quivering beast, ready to use the tattoos and brands on my physical body to bring pain and maybe even torture the demon's spirit form. I could cause all sorts of grief and discomfort if I didn't get what I wanted, and I let the monster know this.

"What do you want?" Golooth cried, and I could hear the defeat in its voice.

"I want to know what we can do to help that woman," I explained, standing over the low-level demon, ready to bring more suffering if need be.

"There's nothing you can do for her. Not yet."

"What do you mean, *not yet?*"

"You need to find her first," he said as he began to lick his hand, looking like a cat trying to clean itself.

"She's in the interview room, right outside my body."

"You know what I mean, hunter. You need to find her soul. She's not in there."

I stopped, and couldn't believe what I was hearing. I assumed Golooth had just done something to her to make her unable to move or speak. I'd never considered the fact that the woman wasn't even in her own body.

"What did you do to her?" I demanded, and reached out to grab the stony skin of the Gorno.

"Please don't hurt me," he cried, and tried to get away.

"Then tell me what you did."

"I didn't do anything to her. I swear by the lights of Heeth. She wasn't in there when I arrived. She was already empty."

There was no way that was possible. If she had been dead when he arrived, she wouldn't have a pulse now, wouldn't be breathing, even shallowly. A friend of mine had died not too long ago and had been taken by a monster, but when the monster was flushed out, the body went back to its dead state, almost immediately started to decompose. This woman hadn't.

"You're going to need to explain this a little better than that," I told him, and ran a finger down the demon's cheek. I could hear the stone sizzle and see it smoke as I caressed the surface. Golooth cried out and I stopped, waiting for answers.

"The woman's soul was removed by someone else, and her body was given to me."

"By who?"

"The Maker," the demon whispered, and I remember that name coming up before. When the demon was in police custody it demanded to see either me or this so-called Maker.

"Who is the Maker?" I asked, because I had no idea who he meant. I'd never heard any other monster mention someone or something called *the Maker*, so I needed to be clued in.

"He's the one who offered the body. He's been doing this a while now. He started off with dolls, and then moved on to human hosts."

"Dolls?"

"Yeah, there are three sisters; Chornaks. They're the ones who've been killing people all over the city. I'm sure you know about them."

Of course I did. I had two bodies in the back seat of my Jeep. It was the thing that had been consuming almost all of my time lately. Those sisters were the thing that had tied me to staying in the city, and now here I was, in my own body, talking to a demon, learning that there was someone else behind it all. Isn't there always someone else behind everything these days? Oh how I missed the old days when I would deal with a monster or demon that had no agenda other than escaping a home planet, or wanting to eat something only the Earth could provide it.

"You know about the sisters?" I asked, my interest sparked as I hoped to get some actual answers from this demon.

"Of course I do. They're Chornaks. Ugly things in real life, but the Maker had these sex dolls so he offered them first. That was a month ago, but they recently started acting like themselves again, eating heads off people they're having sex with."

"Do you know where they are?"

"No," he said and turned, then gave me a curious look and smirked as though he was starting to put things together. "Why do you want to know so badly? Are you working that case too? Sticking your fingers in everything you can, right?"

"You know where this Maker is though, right?" I asked, refusing to answer his questions.

"I do, but why should I tell you anything? What's in it for me, hunter?"

I reminded him why, pushing my finger against the center of his forehead. When his screams ended, I asked the question again.

"You're a bastard, you know that, right?" the demon said, and I moved to cause it more pain. "No! Please don't touch me. I'll tell you everything. Please."

"Then spill it."

Golooth told me what he knew. The so-called *Maker* had offered a body to the demon, and apparently it wasn't the only monster given the same deal. Golooth said there might be as many as one hundred or as few as twenty other creatures in human bodies in the city.

"And they're all like the woman you were in?"

"Yes. The Maker empties the bodies and offers them to us. It's easier to enter and inhabit something like that. Even non-demons can take possession because in a way, they're not really alive."

"She has a heartbeat and is breathing," I said, still not sure how this made sense.

"Without the soul, though, any of us can just enter."

"But why were the Chornaks put into dolls then?"

"I don't know. Ask the Maker when you find him."

"And how do I find him? Where is he?"

"I don't know. I was just given the body."

"What area of the city?"

"How am I supposed to know that? I didn't make a map when I left there."

I was starting to get frustrated because the demon seemed to know so little. Nothing he gave me offered any help of finding this *Maker*, or the last sister. If he expected some sort of leniency, he would have to give me more information that was useful.

"Okay, let's go back and start with the Maker. What species is he?"

"I don't know. I do know he looks human. Could be he's done the same thing with himself that he did with us, but other than that, I couldn't tell you. I didn't ask many questions."

"Well, how did you find out about this Maker? Did you answer an ad in some newspaper?"

"No. I don't even know what that means. It was more of a word-of-mouth thing. There was a rumour going around that someone could get me to Earth and put in a human body where I wouldn't be detected or noticed A whole lot of good that was for me: here I am, in a hunter, being tortured for information."

"And you wouldn't have been caught if you hadn't stabbed

me, would you?" I said, realizing that every day I'd been out and about I could be passing these monster-filled humans and not even know about it. Golooth couldn't give me a clear answer as to how many of these other creatures in hiding there were. When I asked what other species he knew of, he gave me the same old answer of *I don't know*. "What can you tell me that will save you any more pain?"

"I don't know. All I can say is others told me about this gateway I could pass through and meet with the Maker. When I got there, he offered the woman's body and told me it was free of charge, but when the day came, he would call on me."

"For what?"

"He said some sort of revolution. I don't know. I agreed because it's better here than near that shit lake where I came from."

None of that was useful for now, but who knew where all this would lead? The demon was offering everything he could, answering all my questions, but it still wasn't helping me. I needed to know how I could find this Maker so I could help the woman, and find the final sister. I would also put an end to everything the Maker was doing, and hopefully fix the mess he'd made. First thing to do was piece together an idea of who he was, and where he was hiding.

"Okay, I need you to tell me everything about when you arrived. I want details about smells, the layout of his house, the lighting, anything you can."

"First off, it wasn't a house," Golooth started, and went into the story.

The demon had stood at the weak spot. It wasn't even on his home world, but an entire dimension over, on the outer rim of the Wrekth galaxy. There were no other beings around when Golooth arrived and he passed through into this world. The room he entered was dark, and the demon was greeted by an old man wearing some sort of hooded jacket with a leather apron over it. There was little in the way of negotiation, as there was only one human body available. The demon agreed to the Maker's terms and entered the new body. With Golooth's new eyes, he looked around the room.

"It was like a workshop of some sort. There were tools on the tables and there were dolls all around the room."

"So the sisters were there?" I asked, imagining a room full of those sex dolls.

"They were, but not right away. They came in just before I left."

"But there were more of them all around the room?"

"Not like *them*. These were smaller, and looked very different. Some of them were dressed with pants, others wore dresses. Some had shiny, nearly glass-like faces, and others looked to me made of some kind of cloth."

"So, they were actual dolls? Not like the sisters?"

"Yes. Small little dolls, like those voodoo dolls demons are sometimes called to, but they looked nicer, more like people."

I hadn't expected that. The way the low-level demon described things, it sounded like the Maker was in some sort of doll workshop, one that made porcelain and stuffed dolls. It could be he was making those non-living dolls to host smaller creatures that could not handle being in a full-sized human body. Instead of using children, maybe it was easier to use the small dolls. I wouldn't put money down on that guess, though. It was just a hypothesis, which in my books was still better than nothing.

"Does any of that help?" the demon asked and slowly began to stand, sensing I wasn't about to attack again.

"Maybe," I said, not wanting to fully admit that it was more than I'd had. "Do you remember anything about outside of the Maker's place? Anything at all? The slightest detail might make a difference."

"Not really. I was so happy to be in a human body, and not needing to fight against the soul of the person who owned it. You have no idea what it's like, having to live as though you're a parasite in someone, constantly fighting with them so you can have a glimpse of the world they have; just to hear, see, and taste the things this planet has to offer. I didn't choose to be born in the world I was, never wanted to live near a lake made of feces, the sky rolling fire, and how hate is the only feeling the other beings on my planet know. When I first found out about this world, it made me feel as though I could really have a life, be the thing I wanted to be. All I want is to be happy."

"I'm sorry, am I supposed to feel bad for you?" I cut in as the demon looked off into the nothingness of the metaphysical world we were in.

The demon dropped his head, acting sad, like I'd bought it for a moment. Gornoes are not helpless creatures running from a terrible place. They create horror, feed off humans and destroy anything they touch. If Golooth happened to be the one demon from its realm that wasn't evil, it was too bad he was born into a race of monsters.

"There was something else," the demon said, slowly lifting his head and looking at me. "There was a place across the road from where I came out. It reeked of death and flowers. It's one of those places where humans dress up their dead loved ones to put them on display for families to say goodbye before planting them."

A funeral parlour. That's what Golooth must've meant, but he had no idea what one was actually called. That would give us more than a place to start, and I guess I owed the demon one. Not something I liked.

"So now what are you going to do?"

I said nothing. Instead I opened my eyes and said the one thing I knew would be off topic.

"Micro-yeti."

Rouge heard my strange word and I could see her vaguely, through a haze, putting the coin to my forehead. Electricity shot through me and I could hear Golooth screaming again. I hadn't expected it to hurt so much, or hear the demon's scream in my ears and in my head so loud. It was like thunder, felt as though it was going to start making my nose bleed.

Then, it was over and I was blinking the world back into what I remembered it to be.

"Are you okay?" Garcia was the first to ask. I looked over at him, and then to Rouge, who was pushing the cork down into the brass bottle.

"That was something else," I said, managing only a whisper.

"It was damn freaky to see, too," Rouge said. "One second

you were talking like you, and then you would answer or scream or cry out in the demon's voice. Not sure I was ready for that."

"So you heard it all?" I asked, not knowing they would. I'd been ready to come back and have to give them a play-by-play of what was said. This would save some time.

"Well," Garcia said, looking over to the motionless woman. "That thing clearly gave you some clues how to find this Maker, and maybe even the last sister, but what are we going to do about her in the meantime?"

"We need to find what this Maker did with her soul," I said, though that still left a huge problem of what to do with her in the interim. Garcia couldn't very well take this comatose woman back to her cell and leave her there. We didn't even know how long her body would survive without her soul in it. I looked at the brass bottle, though, and realized we needed to think outside the box on this one. We would have to put the demon back in the body.

"You're kidding me, right?" Rouge all but yelled, and Garcia seconded her thought. "We spent all that time pulling it out, now we're going to allow it to go back in?"

"It beats Garcia having to try and explain to anyone what happened to her. This way, it's back to the way it was, for now, and we can move on to figuring out how to end all of it at the same time. We find the Maker, and fix it all."

"You don't think this is a good idea, do you?" Rouge asked, turning to the detective.

"The alternative is worse. So yeah, I second the motion, such as it is."

"Well, isn't this just as fucked as it could ever be," Rouge said, and handed me the brass jar. "I guess you'll need this little shit."

I took the bottle and told her I was sorry. There was nothing else really left to discuss. We had very little choice because we didn't fully know what we were dealing with. I didn't want this woman to die, nor did I want to put Garcia in a tough spot. Putting Golooth back in its stolen human vessel seemed like the only real choice. We knew how to get it out when the time came, so it was what it was.

Forgive me if I made a terrible mistake.

Everything was set as right as it could be by the time we left. The demon was put back into the woman and was she was locked back up. Garcia had no extra reports to write, and we had something of a lead. My body was racked with pain, and my head throbbed as badly as it had when I had a parasite attached to it. We went back to the Jeep. I looked around for something to drink, and found a half empty bottle of water under Rouge's seat. That would have to do. I downed it fast and leaned my head against the headrest, taking in long, slow breaths to quiet the throbbing.

"I really hope you know what you're doing," Rouge said, breaking the moment of nothingness I had been enjoying.

"I never said I knew what I was doing, Rouge, but there is nothing else we can really do, is there?"

"We didn't need to put that demon back in the woman's body. We could have killed the bastard instead, or left it in some freezer. How about throw it in the lake? We could have punished the thing and found a different way to help that woman."

I leaned back again, eyes closed, and shook my head. It was easy for her to say that. It was such a simple thing to speak than it was to act. Sure, we could've done that. I could've sent the demon back to its hell world, or could've snuffed the thing out completely, but there was no saying it would make anything better. In fact, it would've made certain things worse, like Garcia's life, and maybe our own. I couldn't be sure of anything, but I knew when I weighed all the options together, this was the best I could come up with. I again tried to explain it to Rouge, hoping that she would have some sort of faith in my decision, but when I opened my eyes and looked over at her, I saw her arms folded across her chest and a frown on her face as she stared out the window.

"You don't have to like it, you just have to know I will do everything I can to get things back to normal," I told her, and put my hand on her thigh. "We'll find the Maker, the last of the sisters, and get answers on how to save that woman."

She turned to face me, but still looked mad. "There's just something about all this I don't like, Dillon. Do you really think this will all turn out right?"

"I have to hope it will, or what's the point of any of it?" I said, and felt the weight of it all on my shoulders. I sighed and leaned back again. "If I just let the despair set in and accept the shittiness of it, what's the point of it all then?"

"Then where do we start?" she said, and put her hand on mine.

"We take what Golooth told us and try to make sense of it."

"How much of it made actual sense?" she asked me, and I told her what I thought.

This was what we knew from what Golooth told us: The Maker was in some sort of house or shop; it was small, and outside of it was a funeral parlour. That was about all of it, really, but there was something there that could help us. We just had to connect the dots. There was an answer within the words he gave, a path to the truth and the Maker, and we just needed to walk over to it. Where could this Maker be? The city was full of funeral parlours. There was one right down the street from where I lived. We'd even seen one the other day when we were trying to find sister number two.

I stopped my thoughts right there.

"Sister number two," I whispered, and couldn't help but smile.

"What about her?"

"We were waiting for her in Bloor West Village because of what the cabbie said. We didn't know where she was for sure, but he said that was the place he'd pick up or drop off all three of them."

"Yeah, and…?"

"And the area is full of all kinds of houses and stores, but there is also a funeral parlour with a church attached to it right there. What if the last sister is still with the Maker? What if she never left the place where she came through?"

"It's as good of a place to start as any. And even if we don't find him, we may still be able to catch the last sister, draw her in with the two back there," she said, motioning to the bodies in the back seat.

I nodded and we drove off. We decided to wait for nightfall, though. Better to stay more under the radar.

We pulled up into the parking lot of the funeral parlour. It felt like the best choice, since we knew from what Golooth said that the place he'd come from was on the opposite side of the road. Once parked, we stared out at the places in front of us, and it didn't take long to find which one seemed to be where the Maker must bring the demons and monsters through. In between a bakery and a clothing store was a place called *Uncle Knick Knack's Novelties*, a toy store.

"That has to be it, right?" Rouge asked, pointing at the same place my eyes had fallen on.

"I'd put money on it," I said. "I can't believe we were so close to it before."

I could see where our Jeep had been parked the other day, only half a block away from the store. We'd been right there, a few steps away, but how could we have known about that, or the Maker, for that matter? We would've tried to nab the last doll, and might've left without ever knowing about the man behind it all. Things have a way of working out just the way we need them to. It was easier to look at it positively like that. Give it all some of that universal law of attraction stuff.

I pulled out my phone and dialed Garcia's number. I figured I would give him a heads-up to where we were and what we hoped we'd found. I also wanted to see if he wanted to come down and be a part of this. After all, Golooth said the he believed the Maker was human, and if he was right, there would be nothing I could really do to him, not without getting into even more trouble.

"Hello," Garcia said when he picked up.

"It's Dillon."

"I know. I do have caller ID on this thing. What's going on? I'm right in the middle of something."

"I just wanted you to know what's going on with the Maker and the sex doll case."

"Please don't say that too loud," he whispered into the phone. "I'm not alone."

"Sorry. Well, we think we might've tracked down this Maker thanks to what the…uh…guy I had a one-on-one with told me. Looks like he might be working out of a place called *Uncle Knick Knack's Novelties.*"

"That was one of the places on the list," Garcia said, and when I asked him what list, he said the one he'd asked for in regards to places that bought out supplies when *Ethereal Dolls* went out of business. "So I think you're on to something. Is the address 2310 Bloor Street West?"

"Looks like it," I said as I squinted through the window.

"Well, are you two going to—" he started, but suddenly stopped talking. "Miss? Do you not still want to file that report with me? Miss?"

"Is everything okay?" I asked him.

"I don't know. This woman just came in, asked to speak to me about information she had in regards to an open homicide, but she's just leaving now. Weird."

"Is it a case you're working on?" I asked, not feeling good about this.

"I have no idea. She asked for me specifically, but just as I met with her, you called."

"How close was she standing to you when you said the address we were at?"

"Ten feet. Why?"

"Nothing for you to be worried about," I said, and asked him if he wanted to join us. He said he might try later, but he had to go meet with the Chief of Police first.

"If anything changes from now to then, text me and I'll call back once I'm free."

I hung up and looked over at Rouge.

"We may have a problem," I told her, and she huffed.

"Don't we always? What is it now?"

"Garcia was called out to take a report from some woman.

When he was talking to me, he said the address of where we are and the woman left without a word."

"You think it's because of us?"

"Maybe or maybe not," I said, but it really felt like one of those things that wasn't just a coincidence. This gave me a cold feeling, as though we needed to move fast or we were going to lose our opportunity. "I think we need to go into that store right now."

"And do what? The store is open, there are people everywhere. You want to just walk in and ask if they stole the soul from a woman and gave her body to a demon? Or maybe ask if they had three sex dolls they sent out into the streets to eat people?"

"Yeah, sure, that could work. I at least want to get a look around. Grab your blade," I told her, and fished a few weapons out of my bag, including my dagger. I also found an amulet, one that contained two living bugs from a planet made of acidic sand. The amulet was a protective piece that would keep her safe from anything that tried to take or corrupt her soul. She looked at it suspiciously and I told her to take it and put it around her neck.

"Why didn't you use this on the demon in the woman?" she asked, still not taking it from me. "Wouldn't it have protected the woman and pushed the demon out?"

"No. It only protects the body, not the soul. Here," I said, and put it into her hand. "You do that, and I'm going to go and grab a little bait for us."

"Bait?" she asked as I went into the back of the Jeep and cut two fingers off each of the dolls. "What are you doing?"

"Well, I hope that there is enough left in these things to set the last sister off. If *sister two* could sense the body back here, maybe *sister three* can sense bits of the other two in my front pocket. It's worth a shot."

I tucked the fingers into my pants pocket and covered the bodies back up. I got out and looked up and down the street, looking for anything suspicious. Not that I even knew what would be suspicious at this point. Aside from seeing the last sister parading up and down the street in broad daylight, anyone at this point could be a suspect. With the Maker putting Golooth in the woman's body, there was no way to know how many other monsters were walking around in human skins. Golooth said there could be as many as a hundred.

"Are you thinking what I'm thinking?" Rouge asked as we waited to jay walk across the mildly busy street.

"I am if you're thinking you'd rather be at home watching Netflix and eating burgers."

"I'm not, though that *is* a good idea. But what I'm really wondering is if that woman in the police station with Garcia, the one who left abruptly, is another one of those things like the woman with the demon it. One of the Maker's other creations."

"It crossed my mind," I admitted, which was why I figured it was important to get in there and do whatever it was we could. If the woman who ditched Garcia was with the Maker, she could be calling him right now to offer a warning of our arrival. We needed to make it quick, and hope there wouldn't be an army coming after us.

We crossed the street and as we did, my eyes never left the front of the store. I half expected someone to come running out at any moment, some sort of weapon in hand, challenging us before we ever set foot in what was undoubtedly the Maker's place. There were all sorts of toys there: dolls, action figures, board games, and old-fashioned wooden blocks and train sets. This place didn't seem to carry any of the latest gadgets and video games kids seemed to spend so much time enjoying these days, which might actually keep children and their parents out of there.

Rouge hesitated at the door, and I could see her hand go to her belt where her dagger was. I held up my hand to her and shook my head.

"Let's just go in and see what's going on in there," I said, and went for the door. "We can go in together, or me first, and then you, but we don't want to just rush in there with guns blazing."

"Why not? We know this is the place. We were right here the other day, and they even bought the sex dolls from *Ethereal Dolls*. Let's just go in and get this shit done."

"Only thing is: look inside," I said, and pointed out three

people in there. "Those might be regular customers, and we don't want to put them at risk," I explained, realizing it was all a learning process for her. Things like this second nature to me, but what we were taking on now was Rouge's first real case. "Together, or one at a time?"

"Together," she whispered, and we went in.

A small bell jingled overhead, and a woman behind the counter greeted us warmly.

"Welcome to *Uncle Knick Knack's Novelties*," she said, waving. "Is there anything you're looking for today that I might help you with?"

"We're just browsing for now," I said, and looked around the narrow shop. "But we're thinking about a doll. Something for my new niece."

"Well, the stuffed dolls are to your right, and the porcelain ones are at the far back next to the Lincoln Logs."

I thanked her, and we started to look around. The other customers didn't pay any attention to us. We moved around the store, and as we did, I listened closely, used my nose to try and pick up any strange odours, but the store seemed like nothing more than what it appeared to be.

"Wow, I used to have one of these," Rouge said, and picked up a dusty, rose-coloured stuffed pig. "It looks so much like the one I had."

"Do you want it?"

"No. Don't be silly. We're not here to buy anything," she whispered. "We're here to see the Maker."

We continued to browse around the store, looking at a few things, asking the store clerk if they carried items they clearly wouldn't. This was going nowhere. I looked all over for any sign that the Maker or the sister might be there, but I couldn't see a single thing worth noting. We needed to be a little more creative.

"Give me a second," I leaned in and whispered to Rouge. "I think I might have an idea."

I walked over to the desk, holding my stomach and asked her if they had a bathroom I could use. I winced and said that I had a pretty bad bladder infection, and she made a concerned face and pointed to the back of the store.

"You just go right through those doors and it's the first room on your left."

"Thanks," I said, and then told Rouge I would be right back.

Heading to the back where I'd been directed, I looked around at each of the people in the store, paths to get out fast if I had to. The people were all busy shopping, not one of them even looked my way, so I was good there. Walking through the door at the back of the store, I looked over my shoulder at Rouge, saw her looking at that stuffed pig again. I thought she wouldn't be leaving here without that, no matter how things turned out. There was something in her eyes that told me she longed for the toy that sparked nostalgia in her soul.

The back of the store led to a small space with three doors. One was marked *Exit*, one was open and was the bathroom, and the third door was closed and had a sign on it saying *Employees Only*. This would normally be the store's stock room, but I was sure this was where Golooth came through and was given the body of the woman it possessed. I was sure the door would lead to the Maker and his workshop.

I moved to the door, looked back one more time to make sure nobody was approaching, and then entered. My Tincher was already in my hand when I breached the threshold, ready to fight. I took a deep breath, and stepped into the unknown.

The room turned out to be empty, at least as far as people went. There was a large wooden table in the center of the dimly lit room, tools and toy parts scattered across it. There were a few boxes here and there, and shelves lining three of the walls, all of them covered in dolls of all kinds. This was definitely the place. It was almost as Golooth had described, only there was no Maker here, no sign of the other sister. Nor was there anywhere else they could be. There was only one way into the room, and I had come through it. It must've been that the woman at the police station had overheard Garcia and called in a warning. The Maker must've run.

Damn!

Back to square one.

I was heading back to the door I'd come through, ready to tell Rouge it was a lost cause and we needed to go. I was only a few steps away from it when I looked over at some of the dolls. There were so many in here, when there was clearly space out on the floor for them. What was the point of keeping them all lined up on the shelf, then? I moved to the closet shelf and examined some of them, looked for some sort of clue as to why they were there. Was the Maker saving these for smaller demons, like we'd thought earlier? Could they have been used previously and now they were sitting there to be used again? Or was there some sort of essence of the previous host still inside, like the sex dolls in the Jeep? I didn't know the answer, but when my hand touched one of the dolls, a knitted rag doll with red yarn hair, something felt off about it.

The doll was too heavy, and warm to the touch. I pulled it towards me, looking at the stitched face, and tried to figure out what was going on.

"Is there something in here?" I whispered to the doll, and I felt like a dummy while I stood there and waited for it to move or say something back to me. I certainly felt like there was something in there, a monster or a demon from some unknown planet, but why wasn't it moving like one of the sisters had? The beings that crossed into this world could pull rocks, sticks and dead leaves to themselves, they could make bodies or inanimate objects move., So why couldn't whatever was in this thing do anything but sit on a shelf?

The simplest answer was that I was looking for things that weren't there. Maybe I was feeling the things I was because there was a need to make sense of all this. When you stare at something for long enough, you'll see what you want, or when all you do is expect the worst, the worst things have a way of showing up.

I shook my head and sat the lifeless doll back down on the shelf. I gave the room another look and wondered if this really was the place at all. Sure, it fit in with what Golooth told us, but could it be we were wrong? Did this Maker only stay in one spot or did he move around to keep from being found? I didn't know for sure, but I was starting to feel like we were just chasing our tails with all of this. We needed to leave, and try and regroup, figure out who the Maker was and where he was now.

"Dillon!"

I was running before Rouge got the second syllable of my name out of her mouth. Her voice was full of fear and urgency. My heart raced at the sound and I was filled with terror at what I might find when I got back out to the store front. I didn't know what it was that made her sound like that, there was no way to be sure. I had money on the idea that it had something to do with the Maker. We wanted to find him so bad, I guessed we got our wish.

I ran back out into the store, and when I did, I saw there were fifteen people other than Rouge in there. The clerk stood front and center, and three others who hadn't been in the store earlier had hold of Rouge. I looked at her, saw her struggling, but the clerk who'd been so friendly and helpful had taken Rouge's dagger and held it to her throat.

"You calm down now, or your knife is going to spill your blood, and that would be such a waste." The clerk kept her eyes on Rouge, and when she saw the fight had died in her, the woman turned towards me. "So, you're the famous Dillon, the monster hunter. I couldn't believe my eyes when you walked in here. It's an honor to meet someone as prolific in their field as you."

"And you are…?"

"I'm the one you came here to look for, no doubt. I can only guess what you were really doing back there after the terrible acting job you gave. What did you think of my workshop?" she asked, and motioned towards the room I had just come from.

"You're the Maker?" I asked, feeling a wave of shock fill me. "I thought you were a man."

"I'm not. I'm not a man or a woman, but clearly, someone has been talking too much. I'm guessing that's how you found me after all this time." The Maker smiled at me but didn't move any closer. Instead, she stayed next to Rouge, blade against her skin, not allowing me to make a move without threatening her life and safety.

"Let her go and we'll deal with this here and now, one on one,"

I said, and put my Tincher away to offer some sort of proof I would keep my end of the bargain.

"And why would I do that?" she laughed. "Look how many of us there are, and I have your friend here too. Isn't she a pretty one?" The Maker turned to Rouge and caressed her cheek with an index finger. She followed it down to her neck, and stopped at the amulet. "I see you gave her a little trinket to protect her from what I do, but what if this knife just slides right through her chest and into her heart? Will the amulet save her then?"

"Why don't you put the knife down and try me then, bitch?" Rouge growled, and the Maker only laughed at her.

"So feisty, this one. There's a fire in your heart that matches your hair, isn't there? Well, maybe I'll just take that thing from around your neck and make you my next host." The Maker grabbed hold of Rouge's jaw, holding her head still no matter how hard she fought. She stared at her, looking into her eyes, and I wanted nothing more than to run and bury my knife in the back of the bitch's head. "You are a special one, aren't you? I can see something so unique in there, quite different than any other I've ever come across; and not just here on Earth. What makes you so special? What is that hiding in there?"

"So what is it you want?" I blurted out, trying to pull the Maker's attention away from Rouge, and back to me. "What's your endgame here?"

"Oh, am I supposed to tell you what I'm going to do, and then you break free and stop me? Is that how it goes?" she asked.

Well, not really, but it's always worth a try.

"I think I know what you're doing already. I know you have others out there, like these ones here. Humans with their souls scooped out, replaced by monsters and demons from other worlds and dimensions. I've already killed some of them."

"Really? But you're only talking about my first creations here, aren't you? The sisters from Mantia? Oh, I already know about them. In fact, when you walked in here, I was so surprised to see you, so soon at least. I knew you'd eventually find me, once the world around you started to change. But when you came in, pretending to browse, I had one of the others go out and find the last sister. She's anxious to meet you."

I wasn't anxious to meet *her*, especially if she could sense the bits of her sister in my pocket.

"Why were you surprised to see us?" Rouge asked, her eyes narrow and on the Maker. "Didn't your crony at the police station call and give you a heads-up that we were coming?"

"My what?"

"The woman at the police station. The one who called you to tell you we were on our way."

"Enough of this, I think. You're both just prolonging the inevitable here." The Maker turned her attention to the others with her. "You four go over there and disarm Dillon. Once you do, we can all go into the back room and be done with all this dirty business. We have many demons to house yet."

I wanted to fight back. There was an urge in me to let out a warrior's cry and go into battle with each and every one of them, but I knew I couldn't. Rouge was still being held, knife to her throat, and each of these men and women in the room were not just monsters or demons, they were people. I had to assume that they had all suffered the same fate as the woman in whom Golooth was currently housed. So if I fought and killed one of them, even hurt them badly, what was to happen to the people when they were able to go back into the bodies?

"Let's go, hunter," one of the men said, and grabbed my arm. I didn't fight him, or the others who took hold of me and pushed me back into the room I'd just run from. Some of them were laughing as they pushed us along, and I looked over my shoulder at Rouge. She made a face at me, and I guess she was trying to ask what I was going to do next, but I could only shake my head. I had no plan to get out of this. Not yet, at least.

Once we were in the back room, the Maker told the others to move us to the far side of it, along the wall that had no doll shelves. The Maker then shut the door, told one of the women to take my Tincher away. She handed the other blade to one of the men holding Rouge, and told him to keep it pressed to her, that as long as her life was in danger, I wouldn't move, and she was right about that. Afterwards, she walked to the table, where she picked up something that looked like a scalpel, and moved straight towards me.

"There are so many who want to see you and your kind dead, but especially you. You've been on this planet a very, very long time, haven't you, Dillon?"

"Long enough," I said, and left it at that, though I thought the longer I kept this Maker talking, the more time I had to come up with a plan. "How long have you been here?"

"What does that matter? I've been here long enough to know my way around, to set this place up, and to start bringing others over that you and your kind will never be able to detect."

"And what about the people who lived in those bodies?" I asked, hoping that I would be able to get some answer that would help me figure out what to do for all the victims if and when I was able to get out of this situation. "Do you just send them off to some other world, or let them fade into oblivion?"

"I would never let something like that happen to a human soul, Dillon. You don't know me at all. I keep all those humans nice and safe. All you have to do is know where to look for them," the Maker said, and smiled slyly at me, and I think I understood her. I looked around the room, at all the dolls on the shelves. I remembered the way the one felt in my hands and knew where she was keeping them safe. "I saw that little spark in your eye there, Dillon. Did you just figure it out?"

"They're in the dolls, aren't they?"

"Indeed they are, safe and sound for now. Would you like to be put in one too?"

"Why can't they move?" I asked, hoping to get something out of her, because I still wasn't sure I was being told the whole truth.

"Oh, they can move, it just takes them time before they're able to. Human souls are just so young and weak. They have to grow strong, fight, and learn how to move those new bodies they're in," she said, and looked over at them. "They're all watching right now, doing their very best to move, so they can escape. None have gotten away yet, but they all want to; just like the two of you. It's nice for you all to have dreams, even if they will never come true."

At that moment, one of the dolls to the left of me shifted. I saw it out of the corner of my eye, and the Maker noticed it too. She clapped her hands and a smile spread on her face.

"Oh, goodie! Just in time," she said, putting the scalpel down and walking over to it.

"Do you think now is the time, Maker?" one of the men holding me asked.

"Of course it is," the Maker said, and lifted the doll from the shelf. I heard a sound then, soft and weak, but it was close to that of a voice, and it was coming from the doll. "I hear you, loved one," she said to the doll in her hands. "But I need to show these two monster hunters just how dire their situation is. Now, Dillon, you and your lovely lady need to watch this, because before long, it'll be your future too."

I didn't want to see what was about to happen, so I turned my head and saw Rouge was staring at me. She mouthed the words "do something", but what was I supposed to do? We had no weapons, and we were outnumbered. This would be a fool's fight, one we would probably lose.

"Make them watch," the Maker said, and there was anger in her voice. "Force their heads this way, and if they try and close their eyes, open them. If that doesn't work, use their own knives to cut their fucking eyelids off." The Maker caressed the hair of the doll, looking at it lovingly again. "It's okay, my child. You are so strong now. Only the strongest soul can make the limbs of these dolls move. And you are so very strong now. That's not all, though. It also means you will be delicious."

With that, the Maker opened her mouth over the face of the doll, and golden light burst from the thing she held. She sucked inward and the light from the doll, the soul of the human, I was guessing, moved to her lips. The Maker drank it; consumed it; her body shook as the light left the doll and entered her. As soon as I saw it happen, I knew what the Maker was without a doubt. It wasn't the first I'd ever dealt with, but they were never like this. Normally a demon like this, a Sluagh from the Beelz, will just suck out the soul of a human and be done with it. But this one, the Maker, had come up with a more devious way to eat those souls, and cause even more damage by giving the bodies to monsters and demons.

Out of the frying pan and into the fire.

Once the Maker was done, and no more light leaked from what I suspect was a now-soulless doll, she tossed it aside, throwing it down like someone might toss an empty wrapper from a chocolate bar. She shuddered and let out a sound of pleasure that would have been sexy if not for the situation. She closed her eyes, licked her lips, and seemed to enjoy the moment.

"Human souls taste so much better than any other creatures in the universes," she said, and licked her lips. "They're even better when they fully ripen."

"So, you're a Sluagh," I said, and if I could somehow manage to get out of the situation I'd found myself in, there was a way to kill her.

"You are good, aren't you, Dillon," she said, and turned back to us. "You do know your monsters and demons, which makes it a shame I'm going to have to take you—both of you—out of the game. I would love to put you in one of these dolls, ripen you both up, but we don't need to bother with that. What's in both of you is ripe enough for me."

The Maker moved towards us. She ordered her minions to hold us still. This was the moment where I had to make a move, or sit back and die. Since I had no wish to say farewell to this world, I balled my hands into fists and took a deep breath. I could feel the adrenaline coursing through me as the Maker picked my Tincher up off the table and studied it.

"This is a very nice knife, Dillon," the Maker said, and I could see her fingers moving over the engravings. "How many curses, counter-curses and spells are in this blade of yours? Is there something in here that could snuff your life out, or hers?"

"There might be one in there for you. Why don't you give it a try and see what happens to you?" I suggested, and shot a look over to Rouge. This was it. In ten seconds, I would move. The second the Maker was in striking range I would fight back, knock this impostor off of me and end this here and now.

That was the plan, at least. I wasn't one hundred percent sure it would work.

"Oh, I am going to try it out, but I think I will use it on your lady friend there first. I could peel her face off with this. Her screams will be so exquisite. And once she's dead, I'll wear her face before I take this knife, soaked in her blood, and bury it in—"

From behind her there was a loud bang and the door was thrown open. The Maker and the rest of us all looked over and saw a woman there, wild-eyed, and scanning the room. The newcomer was dressed in slacks and a fall coat, a little dirty, but the thing I noticed more was the baseball bat in her hand. It was black, with the end wrapped in something that looked like yellow silk, but I was sure it was the membraned wings of a wren dragon. It was a weapon that would instantly do enough damage to send me, or any of these others, out of our bodies, back to where we came from. The newcomer was all but foaming at the mouth, her teeth barred, but when she spotted me, I saw a smile unfold on her face.

Shit. This was all I needed.

"Who the fuck are you?" the Maker said, pointing at the woman with my Tincher.

"I guess I'm late to the party, but now I want to know who you are," the woman said, and moved slowly towards the Maker.

"I'm nobody you need to concern yourself with if you turn around and leave."

"Not without him," the woman said, and pointed at me. "Dillon is mine."

"Parks?" Rouge said, and it was already what I had assumed. I guess he'd already died of thirst or starvation and had taken a new body. I hadn't expected him to use a woman's body, but it was clever. I'd never even been given the option when I needed to switch. As I stared at Parks, I realized he was the woman who had gone to the police station to meet Garcia, and overheard where I was.

"I'll deal with you later," Parks said to Rouge before turning back to the Maker. "Now, put down the knife, get out of my way, and let me send this asshole back to be judged by the Collective."

"Great," the Maker bemoaned. "Another hunter."

That was enough to get Parks' attention; she'd seemed to forget about me as all her (it was hard to think of him as a woman right away) curiosity was taken up by the Maker.

"You know what a hunter is, that must mean you're a—"

"She's a Sluagh," I blurted out, wanting Parks to know how serious this was. "You can deal with me later. Deal with her first."

There was a moment of hesitation in Parks. I could see it in her eyes as she looked from me, to the Maker, and back to me. I needed him—I mean her—to see that this was bigger than the job she'd been sent to accomplish. I was nothing compared to what the Maker was doing. If she got away, the Maker could continue to do what she was doing: bringing monsters and demons to Earth and putting them in human hosts. I didn't have time to explain it all, but if Parks was even half the hunter I was, she would get what was going on in the back of the store and kill the Maker.

Parks never had the chance, though.

"Stop this one," the Maker yelled to the others, and nine of them charged after Parks, while three continued to hold on to me, and three held on to Rouge.

I watched as Parks prepared herself for an attack, though there was no way she could know what was in those human bodies. I wanted to call out to her, offer a warning, but there was no time. The monsters were on Parks before there was even a chance to speak.

The bat went swinging wildly. Two of the bodies dropped the second the bat came in contact with them. I could hear those monsters scream before a light flashed from them and they were gone. A third one went a moment later as Parks let out a battle cry. Out of the corner of my eye I saw the Maker had clearly seen enough, and used the distraction to get out of the room. I tried to warn Parks, but when I opened my mouth, one of the things holding me covered my mouth to prevent it.

"Your master is ditching you," I could hear Rouge saying to her captors. "She's running away, because she knows you're all going to die here. The woman with the bat is going to win and you're all going back to where you came from."

Almost to emphasize the point, Parks hit two more monsters, who left their bodies in a wave of screams. This seemed to be enough to cause the others to worry, or at least loosen their grips on us. Rouge was the first to respond, striking her head into the nose of one of her captors, then grabbed her knife, the one Parks had once owned. It was in the hand of the monster with a very bloody broken nose, and she pried it from his hand easily. I went to tell her to be careful, not to do anything rash, but she was like lightning with the blade. Before I could even get her name out of my mouth, she'd already slit one throat, buried the knife into the chest of another, as the third cut and ran out of there. She then came towards me to attack my captors.

"You should run," I told them, not wanting Rouge to hurt them. These were still the bodies of humans, ones whose souls were in the dolls lining the shelves. If we killed their bodies, then what was to become of those souls? There were already two who might not be able to come back from what Rouge had done.

The three holding me let go, and did their best to get out of there. One did, but the other two ran into the bat-wielding Parks, who'd already dispensed of the other. The woman's face and hair were wild, cheeks spattered in blood. When the last of them dropped, there was nobody left but the three of us, and Parks clearly wasn't going to just let bygones be bygones.

"Parks, you've got to listen to me," I started, and saw Rouge was already walking towards him with her blood-drenched knife. "Rouge, stop. Put the knife down. This is no time to fight."

"Good, Dillon. I'm glad to see you're giving up," Parks said, and made a move towards me.

"No," I shouted. "You stay right fucking there and hear me out."

"I thought you said this was no time to fight?" Parks laughed at me, and sounded as though she'd lost a few of her marbles. Maybe leaving her to die in a basement wasn't the best idea after all. "Well, I don't want to hear your shit, so it's either fight, or bow out."

"Look around you," I cried out, feeling so frustrated by her sheer stupidity. "You just saw that woman run out of here was a Sluagh, a soul eater. All those people were filled with monsters and demons. Why do you think they fell the way they did when you hit them?"

"I don't care, Dillon. I will end you, and then, if there's something more, I'll deal with it myself."

"ENOUGH!" a small but powerful voice suddenly boomed in the small room. It was a frightening sound that caused me to freeze completely, Parks too, but I had no idea where it had come from. "Parks, put down the bat and help me up."

I still couldn't see who was talking, but clearly Parks did, and somehow she seemed to know the owner of it, too. She put the bat down on the floor, a frown on her face, shoulders slumped as if defeated. Parks walked over to the right side of the room and bent down to pick something up. When she stood upright again, she was holding the doll the Maker had drained and discarded. Now, something was inside it.

"Thank you, Parks. Now, you need to stand down and listen." The doll turned to me, its glass eyes looking me up and down. "Dillon. It has been a very long time. You seem to be causing a lot of trouble lately."

"Who, or what, are you?" Rouge asked, still holding the knife defensively in her hand.

"And you must be his human partner," the doll said, and waddled across the table towards us. "Are you the one who's the bad influence on him? No. He's always been a bit of a dick, haven't you Dillon?"

"Rickler?" I said, though I wasn't sure whether I was right or not. Rickler was one of the Collective, a handler of sorts. He was one of those I contacted with when I needed something from them. It had been more than twelve years since I'd talked to him though, and I didn't even recognize his voice.

"It's been a while, hasn't it?" Rickler asked, and sat down on the table. The scene was comical in a way. Rickler was a huge creature, nearly eight feet tall, and built like a brick wall, yet here he was, in the ten-inch body of a stuffed toy that looked like *Holly Hobby*. "Now, Parks, you need to hear Dillon out on this."

"No, what I need to do is send him off this planet and back to the Collective for judgement."

"No, Parks. Not anymore," Rickler said.

"What do you mean by that? I was sent here to—"

"The judgement has already been made. Dillon stays. And his woman here is allowed to be with him. We are also giving our permission and blessing if she wishes to help him hunt. Does that sound good to you, Dillon?" Rickler asked, and it did. It was actually the best news ever, a weight off my chest.

"No!" Parks cried out, all but having a temper tantrum, complete with stomping her feet.

"Yes," Rickler said, and turned back to me. "You've done a lot for the Collective here, Dillon. More than most hunters. And now, with this business, we need you more than ever. There is more to this than you know."

"Is it the whole rebellion thing I've been hearing about?" I asked, guessing that it had to be. Why else would they have sent Parks after me and then change their minds and send Rickler here to call off the dog?

"It's more than just a rebellion, Dillon. There is a hard pushback against everything the Collective stands for. Beings from every dimension, solar system, and realm are joining together to push against the laws and rules, demanding free reign of Earth and the other planets we protect."

"So, now the rules don't matter for Dillon? We're going to let him get away with killing an earthbound creature, mating with a human, and all the other shit he's done?" Parks yelled at the doll as she slammed her fists on the table. "Why are we letting him get away with all this? What is that going to say to the other hunters? There is a reason we have rules. We have to maintain and enforce order here."

Rickler shook his little doll head and moved over to Parks.

"Parks, you are a dedicated hunter, but this is bigger than you know. Look around you. What do you see?"

"Here? Stupid toys, Dillon, her, and all these people on the floor."

"Those toys there," Rickler began to explain, "aren't toys. They're vessels. That Sluagh you allowed to escape, she has been taking souls out of humans and putting in them in those until she decides to eat them. She then offers the empty human bodies to other creatures. Look at how many are up there. There are ninety-nine dolls on that wall; this one I'm in was number one hundred. That means there are one hundred monsters out there that can blend in as though they are anyone else, minus those that you and Dillon's lady over there already killed."

That seemed to get to Parks. I could see her face as she took in all the facts of what was being said and realized the gravity of the situation. This was a giant shit storm, and she was standing knee deep in the mess.

"What do we do then?" Parks asked, her shoulder slumped a bit more as her body physically showed the final stage of the defeat she no doubt felt.

"Start by burning this place down," Rickler said, and Rouge made a surprised sound.

"We can't do that. Not only is it possible that the places on either side and the apartments above will be ruined, but what about all those dolls?" Rouge said, sounding upset.

"What about them?" Rickler asked.

"Well," Rouge began, her voice shaky as she pleaded her case. "They have human souls in them. We can't just leave them here and burn the place down."

"You didn't seem that concerned when you killed those others over there," Rickler said as he pointed to the bodies on the ground.

"I didn't mean to kill them. It was survival instinct that took over. This is different," she said. "We can't just snuff out all these souls like that."

"You have to," Rickler said, and I could tell he took no pleasure in what he was saying. Somehow, even though he was a doll at the moment, I could read the sorrow on his face. "You humans say it best when you say there is no putting the toothpaste back in the tube. Once those souls were taken out, there's no way to put them back in. Better to end their suffering now, so they can move to the next plane of being."

"No!" Rouge shouted, and charged at the table. "I won't accept that. There has to be something we can do."

"I wish there was. One of the main purposes of the Collective is to protect humans, to keep them safe from a world they would never truly understand. But there is nothing to be done for *them*. It's a mercy you're showing them."

Rouge turned to me, hoping I would have some better answer for her, but I didn't. I was hoping we could save them too, but how could we when even Rickler, a creature older than human civilization, said it was impossible? I told Rouge I was sorry, but if what he said was right, then it would be better to let them go than to force them to stay in those bodies. She didn't take my answer any better than Rickler's, but she let it drop. Sometimes you just have to know when you've hit a dead end.

"So, what about me?" Parks asked, now standing by the door, leaning against the wall. "Do I come back and wait for Dillon to fuck up again?"

"No," Rickler said. "You can choose what you do. You can either come back with me and help there, or you can stay here and help Dillon and Rouge."

"Help them? Are you fucking kidding me? She's killed me twice. He left me taped and glued to a chair for days where I slowly and painfully died. And you want me to work with them? You want me to just act as though we're old pals and none of that ever happened?"

"Yes. There's no use holding on to grudges. You're all on the same side. So, you can stay in the city and do your own hunting if you want, or you can help them. This city is in need of all the help it can get."

"No. I think I'd rather come back," Parks said, and shot me a look that was as full of venom as a snake bite. "If I stay here with them, they're likely to kill me again."

"You know," I began, feeling more than a little pissed at her growing sulkiness, "if you'd just stopped and listened to me, none of that would've happened. But you didn't. Instead, you just kept at me without ever considering the bigger picture. If you stay and help me, or do your own thing, I promise not to kill you anymore. Can you do the same?"

"I'm not making that promise," Rouge whispered quietly, but Parks still heard her.

"See what I'm dealing with here, Rickler?" Parks said, pointing at Rouge. Clearly she hadn't said it quietly enough. "These two don't care about anything but themselves. You can't let this stand. The Collective has to put their foot down or it's all chaos. This world needs hunters dedicated to the job, to the laws the Collective has put out. They're disregarding the rules and laughing at me and all of you."

"SHUT UP, PARKS!" Rickler yelled from his tiny, toy body. He might look silly, but that voice carried the weight of his true size and nature. "This is not up for debate. You stay, or you go. There's nothing in between. And there is nothing you say that will change our minds about Dillon. The ruling of the Collective is final. If you question it, the only one leaving here will be you, Parks. Now, what'll it be?"

We sat in the Jeep afterwards and watched as the store began to glow orange. Rouge pulled out her phone and busied herself looking up other things, not interested at all in watching the destruction before us. I wasn't either. There were a million other things I'd rather be doing than watching a store full of human souls unable to escape the prisons they were in burn. I hated the idea, but if there was no way to save them, no way to get them back into their bodies; what were we supposed to do? I would've preferred to drive away, go home and have a nice, hard drink to make me forget what just happened, but we needed to stay and make sure the place burned to the ground. We were there to ensure the Maker or any of her little helpers didn't come back and try to take the dolls. I'd rather they all rest in some sort of peace, move on to the next plane than be food for the soul sucker, devoured over who knew how long, until they eventually winked out of existence.

When Rickler left the doll, and Parks stormed off saying she didn't want to be anywhere near us, I first searched around for my Tincher, and found nothing. I guess the Maker didn't leave it before she ran. I'd really liked it, too. It wouldn't be an easy thing to replace.

Once we saw it was gone, we went about setting the fire. As soon as the first flame flickered, we went to the surrounding stores and saw they were both closed. We then buzzed all the apartments, yelling that there was a fire in one of the stores and they needed to get out. By the time we got to the Jeep, we could see people on the sidewalk, calling the fire department. They wouldn't get there before the flames did their job.

"I can't believe we're letting this happen," Rouge whispered as the sounds of sirens blared in the distance.

"What else can we do, Rouge?" I asked, but felt more like her than I was willing to admit. Letting them all die in there, unaware of what they could see or even feel, didn't seem good or right to me. Part of the reason I was on Earth was to help humans, protect them from the monsters and demons that wanted to come and live here, from the things that wanted to wipe out humans and use the planet for themselves. Yet here I was, sitting in a car as a store began to burn, one full of nearly one hundred souls about to die.

"I don't know what else we could do, but I don't like this one bit. It feels so wrong."

I nodded and took her hand. "I don't like it any better than you do, Rouge, but leaving them in those bodies, trapped, and possibly becoming food for the Maker, this is a better alternative. At the very least we're not just letting them die; we're allowing them to move on from here instead of being damned. If the Maker gets hold of them and eats their souls out of those dolls, they turn into nothing more than food, their essence and soul just winks out of existence once they've been digested, which could take years of pain for them. That would be worse than this. As hard as it is, I'd rather go this way than being dissolved inside some Sluagh. Sometimes it's not about the good choice over the bad, but the least shitty solution."

She went quiet for a while and the store was fully engulfed in flames. There was a large crowd by the time the first fire truck showed up, most of them with cellphones out recording the blaze. There was no need to stick around, so we pulled out of the parking lot at the funeral parlour and drove away from there. I decided to head to Rouge's house because it would be better than going to mine. I figured we could use the space and comfort of her place over the cramped apartment full of reminders of what it is I do.

"So I guess that plan to move to the country is in the trash now?" Rouge said as we drove along the dark streets. There weren't many people out in the night, and I wondered if it was because it was colder, or there was an actual fear brewing about people getting their heads removed.

"I didn't really think about that," I admitted, and wondered if it was still even an option. Now that Parks would be off our backs, there wasn't really much need to go on the run like that. There was also the fact of all the monsters currently in this city, ones that were in disguise as humans, and the bodies that belonged to all those souls currently burning in the store. Did I now have a responsibility to hunt down each and every one of them? Rickler kind of made it seem like I had to, and that Rouge would have to help me. So, in a way, I guess our plans of escape would have to be put on hold. "But I guess with all the work we have to do now, we're sort of stuck here. Are you okay with that?"

She shrugged. "I guess I have to be," she said after a few moments. "Are you still going to move into my place?"

"As long as I get more than one drawer in your dresser," I joked, and was glad to see her smile at that. We needed to do something to relieve the stress of the day. "You want to pick up the dog on the way over first?"

"That would lift my spirits," she said, and called Sue to make sure it was okay to swing by.

After picking up the dog, we headed home. Rouge suggested we call for Swiss Chalet or pizza, but after the last time we did that and had Parks attack me in the house, I said I'd make her something special tonight. "Let's leave takeout for another day."

We pulled into her driveway with the pup and headed into the house. For the rest of the night we lived normal, quiet lives.

There was no talk of monsters, demons, the Collective, the Maker, or head-eating sex dolls. We just played with her dog, ate some food, watched videos on YouTube, and talked about nothing in particular. It was nice to imagine what average people lived like, even if it would be so brief.

Wednesday

I'd been dreaming about running down an ever-lengthening hallway when a commotion woke me. The alarm clock on the night stand read 4:44am, and I felt like it was an ominous number. I didn't know what it was that woke me, and I sat up in bed and listened, not even sure it was real.

"What was that?" Rouge said. Her voice was groggy and she sounded still half asleep.

"You heard it too?"

"I heard something. Don't know what it was, but there was something banging outside, I think."

Great. So much for the quiet life I'd been looking forward to.

I stood up, put on my pants and a hoodie and went to grab my Tincher when I remembered I didn't have it anymore. I thought about asking Rouge for her blade, but decided not to bother. It might've just been a raccoon out there, digging through the trash, looking for something to snack on. I was just being paranoid because there was no way it could be the Maker. She wouldn't have been able to find me.

Regardless, I grabbed my gloves. Even if it wasn't a being from beyond, and it was a just masked animal bandit of the raccoon type, I could use them to protect my hands from the beast's little claws.

"You want some help?" Rouge asked, now she was sitting up in bed.

"It's probably nothing," I told her, and walked over to the bedroom door. "But we should probably get something to put on top of the bins. It'll help keep the little bastards out of there."

"There should be cinder blocks on both, unless I forgot to put them back on. Or you did," she said, and lay back down. "If they're not on there, they should be right beside them."

I nodded and went out the side door of the house, through the kitchen. I turned on the light before I did, and when I came out I saw both the bins stood upright with the blocks on the top. So much for that theory.

I stood by them and listened, to see if there was any way I could get some sense of what it was I'd heard, and if it was still there. I felt stupid, standing in the dark, listening for something I couldn't even be certain was still around, expecting the worst but hoping for something simpler. For all I knew, it was just a truck backfiring, seeing as I couldn't even remember what the sound was exactly that had pulled me out of my dream.

"Anything out there?" Rouge called out from the doorway, and I nearly jumped out of my skin. I turned and saw her looking at me, wiping at her sleepy eyes and holding her knife.

"Garbage cans are fine," I told her and started to head back to the house.

"Shit. Did someone break into the Jeep?"

I turned and looked down the driveway. I could see bits of glass sparkling in the street lights and cursed. Probably some crackhead broke in because I was stupid enough to leave the GPS on the windshield, or the change in the center console. It wasn't the first time someone had done that to me, but the Jeep was brand spanking new.

"Sonofabitch," I grumbled and walked over to the car. As I got to the corner of the house, I could see something moving in there, and immediately felt rage boil in my blood. The bastard was still in there, rooting around, looking for something to steal. Maybe the prick was trying to steal the damn car. I motioned for Rouge to wait where she was, giving a quick look that I hoped said more than words. I didn't want her to get into it with some junkie who might have a weapon or a needle. I wasn't sure I'd do much better against them, but at least I could replace this body. She couldn't replace hers.

I moved slowly, making each step as quiet as I could. I wished I'd grabbed Rouge's knife from her before heading towards the Jeep. What was I supposed to do against a druggie when all I had was my gloves, and my so-so fighting skills? I wasn't some MMA expert, trained in the deadly arts of some form of martial arts. I was good with the weapons I had, but mainly they did all the work for me and required no skill or training. And none of those weapons would help against a human intruder, unless it was something pointy or thick and blunt.

I was less than ten steps away from the Jeep and couldn't make out who was in there, other than a general shape. It was a person, thin, but impossible to tell age, race, or sex. I squinted through the dark, took another quiet step, and then Rouge decided it would be a good time to call out to me.

"Did they take anything?" she all but yelled, clearly unable to see that someone was still in the car, and clearly she hadn't got my meaning when I gave her *the look* earlier.

I turned my head and motioned her to be quiet, but it was too late. The noise had caught the thief's attention, and it seemed as though they were looking right at me. Oh well, so much for the element of surprise. Guess I would have to deal with this a different way.

"I can see you," I called out to the person inside my car. "If you come out now, I won't call the cops."

There was no movement inside. Whoever was in there was frozen, like a deer in the headlights. I waited a beat or two and then told them again to get the hell out of my Jeep, or they'd be going to jail. Still, nothing.

"What's going on, Dillon?"

"Some junkie broke into the car and is still in there," I told her over my shoulder, seeing as the art of surprise had passed, but I kept my eyes on the car.

"I'll call the cops," she said, but I told her to wait. I wanted to give the asshole a chance to leave. I didn't want to have to go in to the police station and do paperwork when I could just get the piece of shit to leave, and then I could go back to bed. It wasn't as though I'd get any money for the window. If someone is breaking into a car to steal little things out of it, or even the car itself, it wasn't as though they'd have the money to pay anything for the damages they might've caused.

"You hear that, pal? My lady is going to call the police if you don't get out of there. Now!"

Still nothing.

"Did you do this?" a woman asked from inside of the Jeep, and at least now I knew it was a woman. That was something.

"No, you're the one who did it. Now, get out of my car, and we'll talk about it."

The door opened and I could see the shadow of the woman as she moved to get out. "Are you the one who killed them? Killed my sisters?"

Oh, shit!

"Rouge, I need you to go to my bag and get the Thurkk," I said quietly as the sex doll stepped out onto the driveway, backlit from the street lights. She was dressed just like her sisters had been: high heels, short skirt, belly top, but she also wore a little fur shrug around her shoulders.

"You killed them, didn't you? Killed my sisters and mutilated them."

"I did. They're not supposed to be here and neither are you."

"Who are you to say who can stay and who can leave? Someone tells you you're a hunter and you think you can hand out sentences to us? You are no law we need to follow. You're a pawn!"

"Well, when you come here and eat the heads off humans, what do you expect? You think you can come here and just kill, to feed some appetite you have? It doesn't work that way. There has to be someone to stop the likes of you, protect these people."

"I never ate anyone's head. It was my other sisters who couldn't control themselves. I warned them, but even so, that doesn't give you the right to kill us, to kill me, or send us off planet."

I laughed a little. "It gives me every right," I told her, wondering where the hell Rouge was. If this Chornak charged at me now, the only thing I had to stop her was my gloves, and with the silicone skin, I didn't even know if they would work well enough. And from my last encounters with her sisters, I knew how tough they were.

"I should skin you alive, hunter, for what you've done. I should soak the ground with your blood and eat your head right off your shoulders."

"Do it then. If you want to come at me, then come at me and try your luck. I'll do the same to you and then find the Maker and end it all."

"You know about the Maker? Are you the one who burnt our home down?"

"Do you really need to ask that question?"

"You killed all those souls, just to get at the Maker? Do you know how many she has taken? How many of us she has freed?"

"I saw the dolls," I said and heard something bang in the house. It sounded loud and metallic. I guessed Rouge had found the Thurkk.

"That's only what the Maker hadn't already eaten," the sex doll said, and laughed. "You have no idea how many monsters roam the world. You saw those dolls on the wall and you think that was it? She's been doing this for a long time."

"How many?" I asked, not wanting to think about what the number could be, but needing to know. If I was going to have to hunt all these trespassers down, I needed to know what the numbers were.

"Why should I tell you? There's nothing in it for me, unless of course you want to make a deal."

"Make a deal? I'll just beat it out of the Maker. I don't need you," I threatened, and felt my impatience for Rouge growing. She shouldn't be taking this long, unless something was wrong. What if this sister wasn't alone? What if the Maker was already here, in the house with Rouge as we stood out in the dark of the driveway?

"I can take you to the Maker if you let me stay."

"And where is she? In my house, right now?" I said, hoping to blow the surprise out of the water.

"No," the sex doll alien said. "Why would she be there? She's holed up in our other spot. I'll take you there if you promise to leave me alone."

"And what guarantee do I have you will leave me alone, especially since I'm the one who killed your sisters? How do I know you're not going to turn around and try to kill me?"

"I loved them. We three were born from the same sack, but we never really got along. We are bonded by the birth, by blood, but they were not willing to try and be something else here. They only wanted to follow their needs, and lust: to go after the things they hungered for. I tried to tell them to stop, to blend in, but they refused. I knew they wouldn't be allowed to stay. If they didn't control themselves, I knew a hunter would come for us, or I would eventually have to do it myself."

"So, you give me what I want, and you what? Stay walking the streets, turning tricks like a cheap hooker?"

"No. I've met someone," the sister said, and held her hands up to show me she meant no harm. "He loves me as I am. Even in this false body, he looks at me and sees the real me, and loves me. I just want to be allowed to stay here, for now, and be happy."

"No head eating?"

"No. I'm not like them. I know how to control those baser urges."

"Why did you break into my car?" I asked, leaning towards letting her stay. It was a hard line not to cross, but how else would I easily find the Maker?

"I broke in because I came to see you. I was under your car when you left the store. I didn't want to break into there, but I was drawn to my dead sisters. I can't help it. It's an impulse drives me, and isn't as easy to control as the head eating is. You need to destroy those bodies so I can let them go."

I nodded, ready to actually do this. I was about to make a deal with a monster that looked like a praying mantis in real life, but in this new body was a walking, talking sex doll. Well, the Collective did tell me to do whatever it took to do my job and get things done. If they wanted to reverse the decision later, that was fully up to them.

"You can take me to her? What about the other monsters?" I asked.

"I don't know where they are. The others were allowed to roam free. She kept me and my sisters close because of the bodies. She knew we'd never fully blend in. Even when I told her I found someone and wanted free of her, she said I couldn't go, she said nobody would ever fully accept these bodies we're in."

"Why those bodies?" I asked, motioning towards her silicone self. "If the Maker had been doing this for so long, why weren't you given human bodies too?"

"We were at first, but our forms, our nature wouldn't be held within those weak things. These were the only bodies that could contain us."

Made sense, I guess. In a world where monsters, soul suckers, talking wigs, and walking sex dolls were a thing, who was I to second guess?

"Okay then," I said and conceded to her offer. "I guess you have a deal. But, if you fuck with me I swear I will—"

"Die, you head-eating bitch!"

Out of nowhere, Rouge came running from the front of the house, the Thurkk in her hand like a spear. She charged at the Chornak, eyes wild, and I was moving before I even knew what I was doing. This was our chance at catching the Maker. If Rouge stabbed her with the weapon, we'd have to start all over again.

"Rouge! No!" I cried out, and watched the gap close between her and her intended victim. The sex doll also turned, made a sound that was like a scream and backed into the Jeep, throwing her hands up protectively. "You can't do it!"

I was on her as fast as I could, grabbing hold of her free hand with my gloved one seconds before she could stab the monster with the Thurkk. Rouge cried out at my touch and dropped the weapon, and turned to me.

"What are you doing?" she said, exasperated, as I let her go. "I had her."

"No. It's fine. I made a deal."

"A deal? With something that eats the heads off people?" she cried. She went to pick up the weapon, but I got to it first.

"It's not like that, Rouge," I said, and turned to the Chornak. "Are you okay?"

"Are you crazy?" she asked Rouge, and then turned to me. "Is she crazy?"

"No, but she's protective. Especially when it looked like we were under attack," I told the sex doll, and turned back to Rouge. "Give me a second, and I'll explain everything."

So I told it all to Rouge and tried to make sense of the senseless. In the end, Rouge agreed to the terms and thought it was the best choice, especially with the freedom the Collective had given us. At first, I was pretty sure she wasn't going to buy into it, that it would need some heavy convincing, but she took it quite well. We went back into the house, got dressed and decided we'd had enough sleep for the night. It was time to go after the Maker before she could wise up to anything and skip town.

We headed west of Rouge's house. The streets were dark and quiet, very few cars out so early in the morning. The sun had yet to hint at rising when we drove onto the highway, and as we left the ramp, Rouge turned the radio down and looked back at the living sex doll in the back seat.

"So where do the heads go?" she asked the monster, being as blunt as can be. "I mean, you and your sisters are only made of silicone and a metal frame, so where do the heads go they ate?"

"They're broken down by an acidic saliva that we can create from our essence. That's the best way I can explain it."

"So they bit them off and what, slowly devour them in their stomachs? Do you even have stomachs?" Rouge asked, disgusted. I can't say I blamed her. It did sound rather nasty. I didn't even want to think about these silicone-covered monsters eating and then eventually having to take a dump of what they didn't digest.

"Not really. Our essence produces the saliva, which dissolves most of the head so it can be sucked up. The remainder is more *pinched* off than bitten off. We don't really have teeth that work. Apparently, the men who would normally use these dolls don't like hard teeth."

"You seem to know a lot about how the heads are eaten for someone who claims to have never had one," Rouge said, and fully turned around to look at the doll in the back seat. "You sure you haven't had some first-hand experience in all of this? Because, from where I'm sitting, it certainly feels like you might have indulged in a little head-sucking yourself."

"I...no...I've never eaten a human head. That was just them," the monster stammered, and I wasn't so sure she was telling the truth. I started to question the choice I'd made to allow her to stay for the information, but then again, it wouldn't be the first time I went back on my word. If I still felt this way when I had dealt with the Maker, I might choose to do something more like my regular work, even if it meant I was a liar. I'm not a monster dick for nothing.

"How far is it?" I asked as we passed the Jameson exit.

"I've never taken the highway," the Chornak said from the back seat, looking out the window. "All I know is that the place is near Queen and Lansdowne. Just east of there."

Great. I would've been better getting off that last exit, but would take the next and then backtrack to the place we just were. I asked her if the place was a store or a house and she said it was a store, like the last.

"It's called *Curiosa Caravan,*" she said, and then laughed. I looked at her in the rear-view mirror. Her face was an emotionless thing, frozen in a semi-erotic expression with her lips partially open. I asked what she was laughing about. "I guess you really don't need me now, do you? I just told you everything you need to get the Maker. So what do you need *me* for, right?"

Was that fear in her voice? It sounded as though she was really worried I was going to go back on my word, which was funny because I'd just been thinking about the very same thing. Still, I was only thinking about it. I wasn't one hundred percent sold on the idea. It's just better to keep your options open.

"You just do your part, get us there, and everything will be hunky dory," I said, and left the highway.

We drove along Queen, the sun finally starting to peek out and light up the horizon. It would have been a beautiful morning if not for the job we had to do, and the monster in the back seat. Not two hours ago it had housed her two dead sisters, but they were now in Rouge's shed. Once we were done with this, we promised to dispose of the bodies for her. She asked that they not be buried because there would still be a trace amount of them she'd be drawn to, so I agreed to remove the silicone off the metal frame and burn it, and then find a way to take the metal to some place that could melt it down.

"The store is at the corner of the next block on the right side of the street. It will be closed at this hour, so you will want to park on the side street and use the back door."

"Have you been in there before?" I asked, and turned south as we passed *Curiosa Caravan*. I parked four car lengths away from the back end of the store.

"Three times. I would go to see my lover, the one I was telling you about who will take care of me after all of this, and when I stayed out too late I had to go there. I'm not as convincing in the daylight as I am at night."

"So you know the layout, where the Maker will be?"

"There is a room in the very back, just like at the other store. When you go in from the rear entrance, you end up in the workshop. There's also a bathroom attached, and a set of stairs that lead into a basement. The basement is where the Maker sleeps when she's there. Or when he's there."

"Wait. *He?*" I asked, having no idea what she was talking about.

"The Maker is sometimes a man, and sometimes a woman. Depends on the body they decide to use. The Maker changes appearances a lot."

"She's swapping bodies?"

"Whenever she can, or he can," the sex doll said, and looked out the window. "But what does it matter what body she's in? Humans are so hung up about sexual identity. Where I'm from, and for many other species in the galaxies and through the realms, gender is liquid, not something set in stone."

"I think you mean *fluid,*" Rouge cut in.

"Thank you for correcting me. So very human of you," the sex doll said with a mocking tone in her voice. "Yes, fluid. That's what I meant, but you had the idea. Anyway, the Maker, whether man or woman, will not be one to go quietly. She may have already changed her form, but she will never expect you to come here. There's no way she could guess that I would tell you about this place."

"Well, I never hold my breath when it comes to these things," I told her, and I didn't. After all these years on Earth being a monster hunter, I'd learned long ago not to take anything for granted. There was a chance that the Maker was in the store right now, waiting for us, ready to attack. Or, she might've guessed that we were going to find out about this place and found a new hideout. I could assume we would end this easy, a little one-two punch, but you know what they say about those that assume. And nothing these days came easy.

The three of us got out of the car and walked to the back of *Curiosa Caravan*. I had a few weapons on me, tucked in a bag. Not many would work well against a Sluagh, but a few would do well enough to cripple her, get some answers from her and then let Rouge use her blade to send the soul sucker off this planet. Though I did hope to get my Tincher back.

"How deep is this room? What would you say the dimensions are?"

"It's a lot like the other room, only not as long as the other. This one is more of a square."

"And aside from the door we're going through, the only other way out is where?"

"Straight across on the other side of the room," the monster said, after a moment of trying to think if it.

"Okay," I said, and put my hand on the door. I twisted the knob and found it was locked.

"There's a key under the mat there," the sex doll said, pointing to a little brown mat under my feet that welcomed us. I lifted it up and there it was, the key to a kingdom.

"Are you ready for this?" I asked, turning to Rouge, and I saw she was white-knuckling the knife she'd stolen from Parks what felt like a year ago.

"As ready as I could ever be for this. How about you?"

I smiled. "I'm never really ready, but I'm a good actor."

I turned the key, opened the door and we stepped into the

new toy store. It was quiet, smelled like peppermint and rubber balls, but there wasn't a peep from anywhere in there. The silence was good, the dark was not. I felt around the wall, trying to find a light switch to give us some idea of where we were going, when the room came to life with bright flouresence. I was caught off guard as I hadn't found the switch, but the lights came on nonetheless.

"Welcome back, hunter," the Maker said, still in her same body, with another fifteen people around her. I had to assume they were all filled with the unholy spirits of monsters and demons. And judging by the dolls on the wall, she had more than we could have imagined. "Thank you so much for bringing the hunter to us," the Maker said to the sex doll to my left. "You've proven yourself to be an asset to the cause."

"No, thank *you*, Maker," said the monster. It had lied to us. I turned to her, shaking my head as I did.

"So you led us here on purpose?" I said, and smirked. "I was wondering just how trustworthy you were. And you're right, by the way, when you said I'd kill you when you outlived your usefulness, though there was a sliver of me that considered letting you live. That sliver is gone now."

"Too bad you're the one who's going to d—" the last sister began to say, sounding as mocking as can be. Well, that ended when I let the Thurkk I had tucked up my sleeve drop into my hand, and I buried the tip of it straight through the bitch's open mouth. What do you know? Perfect fit.

The doll quaked, and blue light exploded from her face before she fell to the floor. I would grab the Thurkk later, when everything was done, seeing as I was going to be the one walking away from all of this. I had no doubts. Well, I had doubts, but I like to be cocky and stay positive, even in the face of a certain loss.

"Well, now that I solved the case of sex dolls biting off more than they can chew, I guess it's time to wrap this up by unmaking the Maker," I said, and looked around the room. The Maker didn't seem shocked at all by what I'd done, but the others with her, they looked rattled, and rattled was good. "If I were the rest of you, I'd run now, though I *will* catch up to every single one of you sooner or later. But, if you want to stick around for a few more days, enjoy the cool air, and the warmth of the Earth's sun, leave now and I'll see you later."

"Nice words, hunter, but I think you'll see these are loyal creatures," the Maker said, but didn't notice more than half of them, nine in all, had been slowly creeping away from her, moving as if to run. A second later though, as those backing up turned and ran, she saw the loyalty she held so dear was only tissue-thin. "Get back here!" she screamed, and then turned to me when I started to laugh.

"Oh, I'm so sorry for that," I said, offering a mocking apology. "I didn't mean to scare off your loyal customers. Me and my big mouth. Now, for the rest of you, my name is Dillon, hers is Rouge, you're not welcome here, prepare to die," I said with an accent.

"Was that a *Princess Bride* reference?" Rouge asked with a smile.

"Glad you were able to get it, even though the impersonation was terrible. But I do love that movie. We should watch it tonight."

"After we deal with these idiots."

I turned back to the Maker and found she was alone now; the others had left her, and there was fear boiling in her eyes. Her hands were empty; there was no sign of my Tincher, but that didn't mean she wasn't hiding it or another weapon somewhere close by. I stood in place for a moment, waiting to see if she would attack, pull a weapon and try and get the upper hand on me. My pulse was steady, I felt sure of myself in this moment, especially with the odds now in my favour with her little hoard having fled. I might not have anything on me that could outright kill her, but I had my gloves, which I was slipping on to hold her still, and Rouge had a blade like my Tincher that would send the Maker back to the empty world she came from. If we couldn't kill the soul sucker, we could at least carve her out of the body she'd stolen.

When she still made no move forward, no doubt worried about what I might do, I saw her take a step back, and it looked as though she was about to try and run. I couldn't allow that. There was the worktable in between us, so I called for Rouge to take the left, as I went right. The Maker decided not to run after all. Instead, she ran to the table, lifted a long, star head screwdriver from it and raised it over her head as she charged at me. She cut the distance, and I knew I had to move fast to avoid getting skewered by the tool.

The Maker cried out as we went toe to toe. She swung the weapon, and I dodged, reaching for the table myself and finding a small knife that I jammed into her upper chest. She cried out and stepped back, but I was at her again, grabbing the front of her shirt and pushing her backwards into the table. The Maker lost her footing and the two of us started to go down. I heard the crunching and cracking of bones before I even realized her neck had come down on the edge of the worktable, and snapped it. We hit the ground, her neck broken, and yet, to my surprise, there was still some fight in her.

I pushed myself back to my feet as the Maker did the same. Her neck was not just broken, it must've been completely shattered. Her head flopped around like a bobble head on a broken spring, somehow still looking to fight.

"I'll kill you, hunter," she growled, and swung the screwdriver at me wildly, and that action caused her head on her floppy neck to move in a horribly comic way. "I'll suck your soul from your body and take it as my own. I'll kill everyone you care about with your face. They'll curse your name as I swallow their souls."

I couldn't really take her seriously. With her head flopping around like that, she looked so silly. She also couldn't see me very well, so I avoided the attacks easily. And since she was so focused on me, she didn't even notice Rouge walking up behind her. Rouge raised the dagger and jammed it into the back of her skull. I watched as the blade broke out the front of the Maker's face and yellowish smoke drifted out of her open mouth. The blade slowly slid out, the metal on bone making a sound like someone using a singing bowl, and then the Maker hit the ground. She was gone.

Case closed.

Finally.

"Well, that was fun," Rouge said, and wiped the bloody blade off on the body of the Maker. "Now what?"

I looked around the room, saw so many more dolls here and wondered if they were all full of souls too. I hoped not, because that would make another seventy-three souls here at least, which meant even more monsters walking around in human skins. This would be a job and a half still left to do, but one that would take a lot of time and luck.

"I think we have to start off by taking all these dolls and burning them, too. With the Maker being unmade, I don't think we need to burn the whole place down."

"You think these have souls in them too?"

I shrugged and looked for something to put all the dolls and stuffed animals in. There was nothing back there, so I told Rouge to start taking them down and putting them on the table while I went out to the front of the store and looked for bags or boxes.

The front end of the store was dark, so I took off one of my gloves and went into my front pocket to pull out my phone, so I could have some sort of light. When I did, I noticed something move, a shadow, and before I could fully react, there was someone charging at me.

I struggled to get my other glove back on, sure that it was one of the monsters that had run; only instead of fleeing, they'd decided to hide here, waiting to attack. I was proven wrong, though as I saw the face of the attacker seconds before I felt something pierce the lower right side of my abdomen. It was hot and cold at the same time, and I reached down as fast as I could to prevent the blade from going any further, or from it being pulled out and stuck back in somewhere else. I winced, but was happy to see the gloves were working because they had stopped dead in their tracks. Even one glove was powerful enough to do the job. I guess my attacker, Parks, hadn't expected that.

"What the fuck are you doing, Parks?" I asked through gritted teeth, not sure if I should pull the knife out, or leave it where it was. It was so warm, burned more than a knife normally does, and when I took a second and looked down, I saw it was my

Tincher in me. How had he gotten that?

"I'm doing what the Collective refuses to do. I'm ending you, and with your own blade nonetheless," she said, but was still unable to fully move her body or hands. I was starting to have trouble keeping a grip on her with the pain, and maybe the blood loss, but I wouldn't let her go. For my own safety, I couldn't let her go. "I think it's only fair, since your whore did the same to me, and stole my blade."

"So what, you made a deal with the Maker in there? Went against everything you claim to believe in?"

"I don't believe in any of it anymore, Dillon. It's all a lie. The Collective is a lie, and you're a fucking lie, Dillon. You're not here to save the world. You're just another cog in the machine that keeps everything going in the wrong direction. You think you're the hero in the story, but you're not. You're a monster too. You're as bad as the Maker is, as any of the things you hunt. You think you're right, but maybe one day you'll look in the mirror and see the piece of shit you really are."

"Dillon!"

I heard Rouge's voice from behind me, but didn't turn to her. I didn't want her to see how shitty I was doing, how weak I was feeling. I told her to stay there, not to come over. I didn't want Parks to have a chance at hurting her, too. I held on tighter to Parks, knowing I was going to have to do something to save us here.

"You need to stop this, Parks," I said quietly, reserving my strength as best as I could. I wanted to reason with her, hold out that we could all walk away from this, but I needed the Tincher out of me. "Walk away now, and I can forget about all of this. The Collective never needs to know what went on here."

"I don't care about them anymore," Parks said, and I could tell she was trying hard to push the knife back into me, hoping it would do the same to me as it would normally do to other monsters and demons. Only I'm not an idiot. Not only would I not put a curse or spell on my own blade that could sent me from this body, but there's actually one in it to prevent it from happening to me. Still, bleeding to death or being stabbed to death, well, there was no counter-spell for that. "I just want my revenge. And when I'm done with you, I'll go after her."

"You won't get out of this in one piece," I said, and continued to struggle to hold her wrist. "You know I have a weapon that can kill you. It's in my bag, a nice little mallet that will make you blink out of existence."

"A lot of good that will do you," Parks said, and I heard Rouge on the move. "You don't have your bag in your hand, so what are you going to do? No need to answer, I already know. You're going to do absolutely nothing. You can hold my hands here like this for now, but you won't be able to do it for long. You're getting weaker already, and when you loosen your grip, I'm going to stab, and stab, and stab, and stab you until you're little more than pulp."

"But you won't really kill me, and then I'll come and get you," I said, trying to sound strong and sure, but I knew she was right. I was feeling so weak, finding it harder and harder to hold on. If my grip failed any more, she'd break free and then I'd be done.

"You can try and come after me, but it won't matter anymore, you know that, right? The end of all this is coming. The Collective is losing the fight and this world is going to be overrun with all those who've been denied the world you so enjoy. And there is nothing you, or your little whore girlfriend, can do to stop it."

"Are you sure about that?" Rouge said, and stepped beside me. "She can't move, can she, Dillon?"

"Not unless I let go of her."

"Good to know," she said, and raised the Luzilapsa. Rouge had gone out to the Jeep where my bag was and retrieved it while I kept Parks talking. I was glad she'd understood the reason I said it out loud the way I did. "Do you mind if I do this?" she asked me, and I could see the sheer terror in Parks' eyes.

"Not at all. You have a knack for saving my ass," I said, and turned back to Parks. "Do you have any last words, Parks?"

The woman opened her mouth, no doubt about to plead for her life, but Rouge didn't bother to wait for anything to come out. She swung the brass-like mallet straight into Parks' face, which exploded into a mist of red as a violet gas seeped out of the ruined face that looked like ground beef. The mist rose, turned black in the air, and then evaporated as though it was never there. The body dropped, yanking the knife from me, and I felt hot blood pouring from the wound, soaking my shirt and running down my leg. I reached out and grabbed the wall, steadied myself and felt Rouge put her arms around me.

"How bad is it?" she asked, trying to see the wound in the dark.

"Nothing a long bath won't fix," I said, and gave her a weak smile.